Rebecca Steele:
Chasing a Dream

*A Look Behind the Scenes
at the
United States Silver Eagles*

By Joanne Patterson

This book is based on a true story.
All characters appearing in this work are
fictitious. Any resemblance to real persons,
living or dead, is purely coincidental.

*Dedicated to every woman
who has ever had a dream*

Dear Reader,

Many of us have stories tucked away in the archives of our memory. Some life events can be so overwhelming that we tend to hide them even from ourselves in an effort not to relive them.

One night not so very long ago, an old favorite song stirred my memory as I sat in my living room watching television. The song reminded me of a time when I fell head over heels in love with a special man. That one song changed my life and hearing it again changed my life again. The song accompanied me on my path to love. It would come to transform my career. Most importantly the song brought back to me the memory of a most amazing love affair, clear and powerful. The song is the reason for this book, my forgotten testament to love, which was hidden from my own view for the better part of two decades. I never shared it with anyone, but I can keep it a secret no longer!

It seems like yesterday. The ten planes. The desert sun. The man. The smile. The chase. Oh I must stop writing to you now for my heart has filled and my pulse races just as it did back then when I think of him! The whisper of my heart tells me to share my story with you now, so I will.

Merry Christmas! Love you Jo — xoxo

Joanne Pattison
Joanne

ACKNOWLEDGEMENTS

To Kate McGahan, my editor and dear friend who had the foresight, patience and creative ability to take a good book and make it a great book.

To Mark Petitte who presented a male's perspective,

To my team of proofreaders who read and reread as copy was changed and rewritten,

To my friends and family who supported and encouraged me to follow my dream,

And a special shout out to my Facebook friends - I couldn't have done this without you.

Thank you all. I am so grateful.

PROLOGUE

Have you listened to the music in your heart? Really listened? Sometimes it comes as a whisper. Sometimes it comes like a rush of wind that knocks you off your feet. The power of music can trigger memories and awaken the deepest parts of your soul. The love songs you sang at the important turns in your life never leave your heart's memory.

Love cannot be forced. It ripens only when the time is right, when the place is right and when the person is right. Love can be fleeting or love can endure. It can be as shallow as a puddle or as deep as the sea. Some spend their whole life looking for love. For those that don't find it early on, it's easy to give up. It helps to have someone along the way who reminds us to keep our hearts open and encourages us to keep the faith that, no matter what, love can still happen to us. Rebecca Steele is the one who reminds us to never stop going after your dreams. Join her on her journey as she shares the twists, turns and dips of her once-in-a-lifetime love.

This is one flight you will not soon forget.

1
Air Show: Miami

.... Ten supersonic jets stand gleaming in the desert sun. The outskirts of Phoenix, Arizona is home to the famous United States Silver Eagles. These pilots and their crew take their shows all over the country to entertain with aerobatic formations and aerial acrobatics. In a matter of moments the second road trip of the year would be underway.

It's time to go. Each of the ten men, dressed in one-piece flight suits, climb up a steel ladder and enter the cockpit of their individual aircraft. The crew chiefs give the pilots a farewell salute and, one by one, the jet aircraft taxi toward the runway. Within moments, a deafening roar splits the air. The United States Silver Eagles have taken to the sky.

Forty maintenance personnel follow closely behind in a cargo plane. Some of them are already asleep. A few are playing poker. Some are thinking about the long trip ahead, hoping there will be some women around. These are responsible, hard-working men who make the most of everything. When the work is over, it's time for play.

Gather 'round Ladies. The Silver Eagles are coming to town!

Everyone on Miami Beach that glorious day seemed to be talking about the big air show later that afternoon. All I wanted was some peace and quiet as I tried to ignore the hustle and bustle that surrounded me. I focused on the ocean view, trying to calm my mind.

A little whisper deep inside of me kept saying, "Something big is going to happen today." For as long as I could remember, these whispers, almost like nudges, would show up now and then to alert me about something. Most of the time I paid attention even though I had no idea where they came from.

Two couples spreading out their blankets nearby kept interrupting me. Chattering enthusiastically, they were making plans to attend the air show and were brimming with excitement. Eventually I returned to my thoughts.

"Hey Becky," A soft but firm voice startled me. "What time is it? We've got a plane to catch."

Sitting up, I glanced at my watch.

"It's only one-thirty, Emily, relax."

I looked over at the girl on the towel next to me who, despite my reassurance, was feverishly gathering up all the stuff girls take to the beach. Having worked together as airline ticket agents in Nashville for the past two years, we were practically like sisters.

"You'd better get moving," she said to me. "We only have two hours until flight time...or weren't you planning on going home today?"

"Okay, okay, I'm coming!" I laughed as I started gathering my stuff, while tugging at my bathing suit bottoms, which had an annoying tendency to ride up.

"Just think Emily, most people save up all year for this and we can just fly down here anytime we want."

Free travel anywhere in the world was one of the perks that inspired me to work for the airlines to begin with. I thought it was the best job a girl could have.

"If we don't board that plane, you won't be coming down here for a good long time," she said. "You know they'll take our flight passes away if we're late for work." Emily reprimanded me over her shoulder as she made her way quickly to the hotel entrance.

She wasn't about to wait for me. I hurried after her, pausing to tell the handsome couple next to us to enjoy the air show. Meanwhile, Emily had disappeared from view.

The door to our room was open when I arrived back at our room and I could already hear her splashing around in the shower as I came in. I looked at the clock. She was right. We didn't have much time. I hurriedly threw the rest of my things in my worn-out flight bag and peeled off my wet bathing suit. As she came out of the bathroom, I realized how beautiful she was with her short auburn hair and gorgeous green eyes. She won't be single much longer, I thought.

I caught a glimpse of myself in the mirror as I stepped into the shower. My long blonde hair was piled on top of my head. My eyes were bright green too, but only because I wore colored contact lenses. People were always telling me that I was a natural beauty. They might have been surprised to know that I wouldn't be caught dead without my black mascara.

Soon we were ready to head out. We were used to traveling. We both threw on some comfortable clothes for the flight. After grabbing my birth control pills and applying a few dabs of makeup, we were off to find a cab at the front of the hotel.

A cab approached. The driver looked friendly enough as he pulled up to the curb beside us. He had a Spanish accent but was easy to understand.

"Where to, girls?" he asked as we slid into the back seat.

"Miami International," I answered. "Can you please hurry? Our plane leaves at 3:30."

"Oh there's no need to hurry dear," he answered. "There's a huge air demonstration show at the airport at 3:00. All flights are delayed about an hour." That dang air show again! That's what those people at the beach were talking about.

"An air show? You've got to be kidding," Emily said cynically to the driver.

"Nope. I'm not kidding. The United States Silver Eagles are performing! People come from all over the Southeast to see them. They're one of the greatest show teams in the world."

"Well at least we won't miss our flight," Emily said as she opened the window to let some air in. "Whew," she continued as she settled into the seat. "All that rushing around for nothing."

We rode to the airport in silence. There was a lot of traffic. It was a noisy ride with horns blowing and brakes squealing. I had no idea there would be thousands of people attending this show.

As we drove by some of the big hotels and restaurants I remembered working and living here a few years before. There was always good money to be made by bartenders with all the tourists coming into town for the winter. The all-night coffee shop was still there. It was the place where bartenders and waitresses would gather after a hard night's work. That's where I met my ex-husband, Danny. We settled into the Miami lifestyle and into what I thought was a great marriage. I learned from him that things could change in an instant when he just disappeared one day. I never heard from him again.

We finally reached the airline terminal. The cab driver waved his hand to get my attention. He helped get our bags out of the trunk and then a curbside porter quickly checked them through to Nashville for us.

"Where's the best place to watch this show?" I asked the driver as I pressed a generous tip into his hand.

"Well now, Honey," he replied, "you go right around the end of the building over here and you'll see a paved driveway. Walk to the end of that and you'll practically be on the flight line."

"Thank you, but isn't that a restricted area?" I asked.

"Hell no, Miss. Those Eagles dig good looking' women. They'll love having you there. You girls go have some fun!"

Since we had already decided to make the best of it, we shrugged our shoulders, thanked him again and headed towards the flight line.

The cab driver was right. The driveway led to a great spot to watch the show. We leaned on a car, put on our sunglasses and tried to act like we belonged there. The ceremonies had begun. Somebody on the loudspeaker was introducing all the pilots. To our left were eight silver and blue jet aircraft. On each flight door was an image of a silver eagle draped with an American flag. The crowd's enthusiasm was contagious.

Meanwhile, Emily was excited too, but in a different way. She tugged at my arm.

"Becky! Did you ever see so many men in your life?" she gasped. "This is unbelievable!"

I smiled. She was right. The pilots were in their planes ready for takeoff. On the ground there were men everywhere and they all looked so darned handsome in their uniforms! A brochure I grabbed along the way said that these were the mechanics, the ground crew responsible for the maintenance and safety of the aircraft.

Before long the planes taxied out onto the runway. The loudspeaker blared over the noise of the huge crowd, welcoming everyone to the show.

We could feel the tension mounting in the thousands of spectators as the eight airplanes roared down the runway and lifted off the ground. For the next forty minutes the diving planes swooped and performed all kinds of aerial acrobatics. It was breathtaking.

When the show was over, the aircraft all lined up side by side on the ramp and the pilots climbed out of the cockpits, smiling and waving to the crowd. The cheers and applause were deafening.

I turned to Emily. "It was definitely worth the delay, don't you think?"

She nodded and then poked my arm. "Watch it! There goes your ticket!"

Sure enough, my boarding envelope was gently sailing across the ramp. I took off after it. I couldn't afford to lose it. Lucky for me, one of the Silver Eagles saved the day by stomping on it with his boot. He picked it up and when he noticed me scurrying towards him, a charming smile crossed his face.

"Lose something?" he asked, handing me the envelope.

"Yeah, thanks!" I replied. "The show was amazing and I didn't even realize I had dropped it." This guy was so handsome I was stunned. I caught my breath and tried not to stare.

"Well, I'm glad you enjoyed the show." He smiled again as he made eye contact with me. He then turned and headed toward the airplanes. My face felt flushed.

Emily walked up close behind me.

"If I didn't know you so well, I'd think you did that on purpose," she said with a twinkle in her eye.

"Did you see him Emily?" I asked, still staring after the handsome man.

"Sure. I saw him. So what?" she answered. "Do you have any idea how many girls all over the country are probably madly in love with him, as well as with the rest of these guys? They've got girls in every port, you can bet on that."

"You're probably right," I answered, sighing.

The huge crowd had moved forward onto the ramp to get autographs. Apparently this air show was a very big deal.

"Come on, let's go catch our flight," Emily called over her shoulder. "There's nothing I'd rather do than go back to work!" she said, tossing her head and laughing sarcastically.

We checked in at the ticket counter and managed to get the last two seats on the plane to Nashville. Because we were airline employees, we always had to wait until the end to board and hope there were available seats. Luck was on my side again. As I found my seat and fastened my seatbelt, I remembered my thought from earlier in the day...the thought that something big was going to happen. I asked myself again, what could it be? There was no way I could have possibly known that it had already happened.

In no time at all we found ourselves on the final approach to Nashville. It was always exciting to come home.

2
Air Show: Nashville

The landing gear jolted us when we hit the tarmac. I sat up, slowly stretching and noticed that Emily was staring out the window.

"Weren't you able to sleep? What's going on?" I asked her.

"I couldn't stop thinking about those handsome Silver Eagle guys. Wouldn't it be fun to go to a party with them? You'd almost be guaranteed to find someone you liked."

"Dream all you want, Em, but the odds of seeing them again are pretty slim." As I said this, I got to thinking I wouldn't mind seeing the air show again, or that handsome guy for that matter.

We eventually deplaned, picked up our luggage and drove home. We both lived in the same apartment complex a few miles from the airport and it was great to be so close to my best friend and to work. When I arrived home it felt good to be there, back in my own bed. Nonetheless, thoughts of going to see the Silver Eagles again kept slowly creeping into my mind.

The night passed quickly and Emily called me first thing the next morning.

"You won't believe what I just found out!" She was very excited. "The Silver Eagles are in town for an air show tomorrow!"

"Emily, you're kidding, right?" I responded with surprise and delight.

"Nope. A bunch of us are going over to the hotel for the big welcoming party tonight."

"Thanks for letting me know, Emily! Count me in! I'll see you later."

Off I went to buy something new and fun to wear. As the day passed I couldn't help but wonder: Would the handsome guy from the Miami show be here? What would be the odds of that? But then again, what were the odds that they would be performing here in my own hometown tomorrow? It's all I could think about all day long.

Later that evening, several carloads of friends met at the front door of the club because we all wanted to walk in together, the way women like to do. As we entered the dark and expansive room, we could tell that the central bar area was jammed. It looked like a sea of men! We threw our jackets onto a pile near the front door and ventured in.

I was relieved that I knew the barmaid. It pays to know the right people in life. I called out to her hoping she could hear me over the noise of the crowd.

"Hey Donna! Are there any places left at the bar?" I asked her, shouting over the noise of the crowd.

"Come on over to the other side, Becky," she hollered back at me. "I'll make room for you."

We pushed our way over to the far side of the bar. I kept my eyes averted, too shy to look around. What if that guy from Miami is here? I had spent most of the day thinking about him, imagining what it would be like to see him again. Oh dear, but what if he is here with someone else? I felt a real attraction to him but I knew I wouldn't be able talk with him unless he was by himself.

Soon we were seated comfortably and Donna took our drink order.

I leaned over the bar. "Wow Donna, are these guys all Silver Eagles?"

"Yup," she replied, "they sure are. I've already got dates lined up with two of them after work tonight. I'll probably go with Joe though. I kind of like him."

I shifted in my seat, a bit taken aback. Donna was a nice person and all but she was old enough to be a grandmother to most of these men.

Emily nudged me. "Don't be so surprised," she said under her breath. "Rumor has it that she has a reputation of sleeping with younger guys."

A few of the men clustered around us at the bar. We found that it very easy to be with them because they were so polite and sociable. Within minutes they were talking and laughing with us as if we had all known each other for years.

"Looks like you can pretty much take your pick, Becky," Emily commented to me out of the side of her mouth. "You don't see many girls around here, do you?" The odds were good.

It was fun talking with the guys. What a pleasant surprise it was to see that they were not at all like the wild reputation we had heard they possessed. I kept glancing around, mostly to see if the guy with the smile was there. A lot of men were swarming around us but even so, I kept thinking about him, looking for him. Would I recognize him if I saw him? I remembered that his name was stitched into his uniform shirt that day. I wished I had paid more attention to it. I had been too busy looking at him...and his smile.

"You girls can fly all over for free, can't you?" One of them had approached me from the far end of the bar.

He extended his hand. "Hi, my name's Paul."

I shook his hand and introduced myself.

"Yes, Paul," I added. "We can fly pretty much anywhere."

"Tell you what," he proposed, "How about dropping me a line in Phoenix? It's my home base. Maybe the next time you're on leave, you can fly out to see me." Before I had a chance to answer, he continued, "I sure would like to spend more time with you here, but we've got an early bus call in the morning and we have to be up at the crack of dawn."

I glanced around the club. The place suddenly seemed to be clearing out in a hurry. I looked back at Paul who was quickly scrawling his address and phone number onto a cocktail napkin.

"Will you do that Becky, will you come to Phoenix?" he whispered, almost pleading.

"Sure Paul," I said, rather nonchalantly. "Why not?"

"Good," he answered. "I'm glad. See you soon."

He leaned over and kissed me on the cheek.

"Goodnight Darlin'," he murmured in my ear.

I said goodnight to him and looked around. As if on cue, all of the Silver Eagles had left the bar at the same time.

Emily and I decided to leave then too. The reason we had come was gone and we both had early shifts the next morning. Most of the other girls had already left. Our two coats were the last remaining coats on the table.

As we stepped outside Emily asked eagerly, "So are you going to write to him, Becky, are you?" She could hardly wait for my answer. She could hardly stand still.

I answered, "I think so. Why not? I can't think of a reason why I shouldn't."

Meanwhile in the back of my mind, I really never thought I'd hear from Paul again. He was pretty smooth and I was sure lots of other girls had those paper napkins. It was late and the morning would come all too early. We went home and I spent the night in dreamless sleep.

The next day unfolded perfectly. Emily and I were working the same shift. All the scheduled afternoon flights had been delayed, so we were able to watch the air show from the airport's observation deck. It was just as exciting the second time around. Emily and I felt privileged that we were able to see the show again so soon.

As soon as it was over, I became intent on watching all the men who were a part of the Silver Eagles show team. I was looking for him, the charming man with the boyish smile. The pilots were introduced but he was not among them and neither was Paul. I was soon to find out that Paul was not a pilot at all but was part of the maintenance team. I tried and tried to find the handsome man but sadly realized he wasn't there. Why would I tell Paul that I would fly to see him in Phoenix when all I wanted was to meet that handsome guy with the great smile? The whisper inside me was telling me not to worry, that it would all work out somehow.

All of a sudden I realized that "the big thing" that was going to happen in Miami was my chance encounter with this handsome man. The universe works in mysterious ways. Maybe Paul was just a stepping-stone to get to him. I knew I had to take that chance. If Paul were to call me, I would have no choice. I would have to go.

3
Air Show: Pittsburgh

A few days went by with no word from Paul. I wrote him a letter and called his apartment but I couldn't seem to reach him. I was hoping he hadn't forgotten about me.

One night the phone rang. I looked at the clock. It was two a.m. and I was a little nervous. Who would be calling at this hour? As I picked up the receiver I recognized the hum of a long distance call. Much to my surprise, it was Paul calling from Texas.

"Hi Babe. Wanna' meet me in Pittsburgh next Thursday for the weekend show?" I was sure he could hear my excitement as I agreed to meet him at his hotel the day before the show.

"Great," he said, "It's a date."

As I hung up the phone, I couldn't help but wonder if I was beginning a new chapter in my life. Would the guy with the charming smile be there? I had no idea how this would work out if he was, but I was absolutely confident that it would, somehow.

When I arrived at work the following morning, I checked the flight schedule to

Pittsburgh. Flying there from Nashville was a snap. I arranged for the time off and before I knew it, I was on my way. Emily had made a point of telling me to have fun but she cautioned me to be careful at the same time. After all, she would not be there to chaperone me. She was wishing she could come along.

I rented a car in Pittsburgh and drove to the hotel. I was surprised to find that the Silver Eagles had not yet checked in. All the hotels in the area were sold out because of the air show. I had no other choice. The only place available in town was Paul's room, so I simply said I was his wife and no one behind the desk batted an eyelash.

A few minutes after I arrived at the room, the bedside phone rang. It was Paul calling to ask me to pick him up at the airport. He was relieved that I had arrived on time like we had agreed. I hoped I would recognize him. It was difficult to remember what he looked like in the smoke-filled bar that night.

I didn't need to worry. He remembered me immediately and greeted me with a big bear hug. He flung his bag over his shoulder and off we went to the hotel.

As soon as we got back to the room, he received a phone call from someone in Phoenix. He was on the phone for a long time.

19

I didn't know what to do with myself and I found myself getting disillusioned. After flying all this way, I didn't feel like I was a priority to him.

By the time we headed downstairs to the bar, I was ready for a drink. I now felt uneasy with him. I hoped the alcohol would take the edge off. We found a corner booth by the door. Paul went up to the bar to order drinks. He was there for a while talking with someone so I had plenty of time to look around. There were a lot of good-looking men standing at the bar. Most of them looked pretty bored. If only Emily and the girls were here, I thought, these guys would not be bored another minute!

When Paul finally brought our drinks over, he brought someone with him. "Becky, I'd like you to meet my roommate from Phoenix, Johnny Munroe."

I glanced up and as I started to say hello, I tried not to choke. My voice got stuck in my throat on the way. It was him! It was the handsome man with the great smile. Wow, it was him!

Johnny Munroe slid into the booth across from me, grinning.

"Lost any tickets lately?" he chuckled.

I tried not to stare at him. I was glad to finally know his name. Johnny. Johnny

Munroe. Could it be that he was sitting right across the table from me? Was he really here? It felt like a dream. My heart was pounding. This was an incredible turn of events. It was unbelievable. It was wonderful...except for one thing. I was still with Paul. I was on a date with Johnny Munroe's roommate.

"I'm surprised you recognized me," I managed to say to him.

"I never forget a good-looking girl, especially when her ticket lands at my foot." He smiled, watching me intently. It felt like a movie. I was sure this was fate. How else could this have happened?

Soon we were all laughing and I was finally able to relax, while the attraction between Johnny and me sizzled in the air. It seemed I needed some kind of a miracle to turn this situation around. Paul had asked me to come, so for the moment I was stuck with him. I didn't have much choice.

After a few more minutes, Johnny put his empty glass on the table, said goodnight and went upstairs. We finished our drinks and were right behind him. I glanced over at Paul. I wondered if he could tell I was attracted to Johnny. Could he sense that I wanted to be with Johnny instead? There had to be a way out of this.

21

As we entered Paul's room, I realized there was one thing in my favor. There were two beds. I later learned that Paul's roommate (was it Johnny?) had found another place to stay in order to make room for me. Apparently these guys put a lot of thought into these things. There were a number of arrangements the men would make to accommodate each other when they were traveling if there were women involved. I was learning about it firsthand.

There seemed to be some distance between us now. I was kind of glad for the space because seeing Johnny again changed everything for me. I wondered if Paul's change in attitude was the miracle I'd been hoping for. After some brief and shallow conversation, I fell down onto the bed exhausted and slept there in my clothes all night. Shoes and all.

4
The Dream Begins: Pittsburgh

Paul was friendly but distant the next morning. I had so many questions. Was he disappointed that we hadn't slept together? I figured there must be more to it than that. It was uncomfortable to be in a room with a stranger. I spent as much time in the bathroom as possible, more or less hiding out.

That afternoon we left for the airport and I was excited about seeing the air show again. We had a Silver Eagle car pass so we could park right on the ramp near the flight line.

The show was breathtaking and I felt very patriotic as the shiny jets performed their maneuvers. I sat on the hood of the car and looked around at all the men, forty or more of them, in uniforms wearing the Silver Eagle logo so proudly. Mostly I was looking, yes searching, for Johnny. Where was he? How would I find him? Every one of the men was good-looking, attractive and clean-cut. It seemed as if they had to fit a certain image to be a Silver Eagle. Emily sure was right when she said they must have girlfriends all over the country.

As soon as the show was over, I was relieved when Paul hurried away to check out a problem with one of the planes. He had hardly looked at me since the night before and I guessed he was sorry that he had invited me.

"Did Paul leave you all alone?"

Johnny had appeared like magic, out of nowhere. I gazed into his smiling face. How did he find me in this huge crowd of people?

"Paul had to go to work on one of the planes," I reported.

He then sat down next to me. "Can't wait to have a beer tonight. It's been a rough day. Wonder if there'll be any girls around." He frowned, "Last night sure was a dry run."

"Why on earth would a good-looking guy like you have any problem finding a girl?" I asked.

He just laughed it off and said he hoped he'd have better luck than the night before. "I wish I could talk with you longer but I better get back to work before somebody misses me." He stood up and put his hand on my arm for a moment. He then thought better of whatever it was he wanted to say and walked away. As I watched him stroll over to the mechanic's trailer, I thought how proud I'd feel to be his girl. He walked by me once more a few minutes later, called out "Smile!" and was gone again.

Paul eventually came back to the car, handed me the keys and said that I might as well go back to the hotel without him. He still had a lot of work to do. As I drove back to the hotel, I made tentative plans to leave in the morning.

It was very late when Paul returned to the room. When he finally did, I was waiting up for him. He said he wanted to tell me something.

"You've made quite a hit with all the guys you know," he started. "They're fighting each other to stand in line for you..."

"I guess that's a compliment," I replied to him, forcing a smile. It was obvious he had more to say. I didn't like him much at this point. This trip wasn't turning out the way I'd imagined.

He told me the whole story. The girl on the phone the night before was his fiancé. He loved her and was going to marry her. He admitted to me that he should never have asked me to come to visit him.

"I was drunk and you were just...so pretty. All the guys want you. You can have your pick," he said. "You have plenty of reasons to stay if you don't want to go home tomorrow." What did I want? It was my chance, my chance for a miracle. I was honest with him. I told him the only man I found attractive was Johnny.

"Would you be willing to call him and ask him if he wants me to stay? If he does, then maybe I will. Maybe I will stay. Can you call him?" I looked at him expectantly.

"Call him? Now? Are you crazy? Do you know what time it is?" he glared at me. I knew what time it was. It was 4:15 in the morning and I was losing my patience. After all, Paul had been stringing me along the whole time.

"Yes, I know what time it is," I said bluntly. "You asked me to come here and now you tell me this. It's the least you can do for me, don't you think?"

"Okay, okay, I'll call him," Paul said begrudgingly.

I closed myself in the bathroom so that I could have some privacy. So many thoughts flooded my mind. I could hear their conversation through the paper-thin walls. I desperately wanted to stay but was scared to death that Johnny wouldn't want to be with me.

"Johnny listen," Paul was saying, "...yeah, yeah, I know what time it is. Hey man, I need some slack. Things have changed over here...no, not tonight, tomorrow. Becky says she'll stay, but only if you want her to."

My heart was beating so loud I could hardly hear the rest.

What did "slack" mean?

"Okay, I'll tell her. See you later."

I opened the door cautiously. "Well, what did he say?"

"He said he'll call you in the morning." My face fell. They always say they'll call you and then they never do.

"...He said he wants you to stay."

As simply as that he turned over in the bed, leaving me with a head full of questions. I could hardly contain my joy.

What was I doing? What if Johnny was just like all the rest of these men? I guessed there was only one way to find out. I glanced over at Paul, already snoring in the bed next to mine. What a disappointment he turned out to be.

The phone rang about an hour later. It startled me and Paul grabbed it like a first responder. "Yeah, Johnny, she's right here." He handed the phone to me.

"It's him," he said, and promptly rolled back over again. He could've cared less. I could not imagine why Johnny would be calling me at 5 am.

"Hi and good morning, Beck." My name rolled off his tongue as if he said it every day. He wanted to know if I could get more time off from work. "Don't you want to stay a little while longer?" he asked.

I said yes, hoping I was doing the right thing.

"Good," he said. "I'll call you when I get up, okay?"

I could imagine his smiling face as he said, "Hey, I almost forgot... smile!" as he hung up the phone. Everything had changed in an instant. Life is like that sometimes. When I closed my eyes I had the biggest smile on my face.

The phone caught me off guard the next morning. I guess I never really thought Johnny would call. "Come on, I'll meet you down by the pool in twenty minutes!" he said cheerfully.

I said a happy "okay," took a shower, put on my bathing suit and headed to the pool. I had just settled into a comfortable lounge chair when Johnny appeared. He looked even better than I remembered from the night before. He handed me his room key and told me to move my stuff to his room whenever I felt like it. What was this anyway?

They just assume that women will stay with them?

I asked him about his roommate. "What happens to him?"

"Don't you worry about anything," he responded. "This happens every trip. I'll take care of it." I paused to look at him and wondered what he meant by that remark. The truth about these road trips was staring me in the face and yet I chose to ignore it. It was obvious that this was not a big deal to him. I remembered the empty bed in Paul's room. These guys took good care of each other. Does "pulling slack" have something to do with the way they figured out the room arrangements?

After a short time at the pool, Johnny and some of the others had to leave for work. He told me to just relax, enjoy the sunshine and have a great afternoon. I was certainly happy I had chosen to stay. I thought it would be a good time to get my things from Paul's room. I hoped that no one would see me, since I had said I was Paul's wife! I didn't want to have to come up with an explanation for what I was doing now.

My wish for a miracle had come true. I was with Johnny now. Once again I remembered that day in Miami when I was so sure that something big was going to happen.

Could it be that I was destined to meet
Johnny?

5
Learning The Ropes: Pittsburgh

After gathering my things from Paul's room, I found my way to Johnny's room and opened the door. Wow what a mess! I put all my stuff in a safe corner of the closet.

Johnny called and wanted to know if I was glad I stayed. I told him I wasn't sure yet, but that I thought things were looking up. He arrived back to the hotel within the hour. His roommate walked in behind him carrying two six packs of beer. "Room service!"

Johnny laughed. "Becky, meet Mike, Mike Bronson." I recognized his roommate as the man who kept walking by and staring at me the day before. His blond hair and blue eyes made him easy to remember. All these guys looked like movie stars.

Johnny then took my arm and propelled me toward the door. "Come on, let's go downstairs for a drink."

We sat in a booth with his buddy, Slim, and his girl, Carol. He explained that they were close friends, part of a group of four that frequently hung out together.

Johnny was easy to talk to. He told me that he wanted to be with me when he first met me but that he would never compete for his friend's girl. Then he started explaining the events of the night before.

"I'm sorry I couldn't be with you sooner but I had a hammer in my room when Paul called. Didn't you know that?"

"What's a hammer?" I asked innocently.

"A hammer is a girl, silly. That's why I couldn't talk."

Trying to understand their lingo would be difficult without some explanation. It was much like a code.

"Johnny," I said, "if we're going to be together, please, I have to understand what you're saying."

"Okay, Becky, the next time I say something you don't understand, just ask me and I'll explain it to you." He squeezed my hand and smiled. He was very charming and I was starting to like him more and more.

Slim and Carol eventually got up to leave and said goodnight. They were polite and all, but I got the feeling they didn't think I was going to be around for long. I wanted so much to believe they were wrong.

About midnight Johnny decided to go

upstairs to change his clothes. Oh no, I thought, is he trying to get me to go upstairs with him? My question was quickly answered.

"Wait here for me, I'll be right back," he whispered as he got up from the table. He was back in less than ten minutes.

"Come on, Honey," he said, "you haven't been out on the town since you've been here. We're going out!" Off we went to a swinging place down the road called Foxy's. The band was so loud it was almost impossible to talk.

"Boy the boys are really firing, aren't they?" Johnny said over the roar of the music. This was my next lesson in Silver Eagle slang.

"What does that mean?" I asked, tugging at his sleeve. He kind of looked surprised that I didn't know, but he explained.

"Firing, you know, like trying to get a girl to sleep with you. We call it firing your best shot. Remember that." I filed it in my brain under Silver Eagle slang and turned my complete attention to Specialist Johnny Munroe. Johnny was about five foot nine or so, weighing in I guessed at about 180 pounds with dark brown hair and deep brown eyes. He was definitely good-looking, in a rugged kind of way, but what I liked the most about him was his smile. It was his smile that had won me over.

"You realize I picked you out of all the guys, don't you?" I said as I moved closer to him.

"I know that," he answered. "...And I don't want you to be disappointed."

I replied with a smile.

"I like it when you grin at me," he said grinning back.

"That sounds like your best shot," I laughed, already picking up the lingo. Then I took a deep breath. I had to ask..."Johnny, are you married?"

"No dear, I'm not married. Never have been either. I only intend to get married once and when I do I won't be running around on my wife." He looked at me intently while he spoke to me. He was so tuned in and sensitive that he hypnotized me. It seemed that he looked straight into my soul with those deep brown eyes.

We stayed there until the place closed down and then we came back to the hotel. I'm sure the drinks helped to relax me. There was no doubt we were going to make love. When he pulled back the sheets of the bed and beckoned to me, I slid in beside him. For a moment we just looked at each other. His face seemed vaguely familiar. Comforting. I touched his cheek and gazed into his eyes. My senses were alive. His skin smelled like my father's aftershave. He pulled me close and kissed me, softly at first. I felt like I had come home. It was not long before passion overtook us and there was nothing beyond the two of us. Making love with him was breathtaking and beautiful.

When we relaxed after most of the night was over, we clung to each other, afraid if we let go we might find that it was only a dream. Being with Johnny moved me. Little did I know I would never be the same again.

At last, he opened his eyes and looked at me. "Wow," he said breathlessly, "Thank goodness you didn't go home."

He held me close for a few moments and then we both drifted off to sleep, wrapped in each other's arms.

6
Final Day: Pittsburgh

The phone rang first thing in the morning but instead of reaching for it, we reached for each other. It rang about ten times before Johnny finally picked it up. I was learning to hate telephones. They always seemed to ring at the wrong time. Mike was calling.

"Sure come on up...oh never mind why I'm out of breath!" Johnny slammed down the receiver.

"Lame bastard," he laughed, "He's my best buddy though. Never met another guy like him, that's for sure." He explained that he and Mike always shared a room when they traveled together.

A few moments later Mike unlocked the door and walked in. There I was with just a sheet pulled up practically over my head. I found, however, that I had no reason to be embarrassed at all. Mike greeted me and was very nonchalant about my being there, as if this kind of thing happened every day. I stayed in bed taking it all in as they both showered and got ready for the workday. As they were leaving, Johnny gave me a quick kiss and said he'd call me as soon as he knew what time they would be back.

After they left, I lay there quietly for a little while and contemplated the last 24 hours. I was caught in a whirlwind of emotion. I felt like I was hanging on by my fingertips. Johnny called me around noon to let me know that they would be back in a couple hours. The show had been cancelled due to a low cloud cover. The new plan was to go out by the pool and drink screwdrivers.

Johnny and Mike, along with two others, arrived back at the room at the same time. We all sat around making small talk for a few minutes. Everyone seemed anxious to get down to the pool so I grabbed my stuff too, assuming Johnny and I were going too.

"Go ahead, fellows!" he said. "We'll be down in a minute." He took my hand.

"I hope you have a heart attack you son of a bitch," Mike said to Johnny as he threw his head back in laughter and slammed the door behind him. I smiled at Mike's comment for I had quickly come to understand the way he and Johnny teased each other.

The moment the door closed, Johnny reached for me.

"I thought we were going down to the pool," I whispered as he pulled me to him.

"Who's the boss here?" he asked in his huskiest voice.

We made love quickly. I was totally smitten. I could feel myself falling for him. Johnny smiled at me as I rolled over and got out of bed with the sheet wrapped around me.

"Give me five minutes for a quick shower!" I called out on my way to the bathroom. "I'll meet you down by the pool."

I heard him say, "Okay, but hurry up," as he closed the door behind him.

By the time I got downstairs, there must have been thirty men sitting around the pool drinking beer and relaxing. Johnny was watching for me and readily took my hand as I walked into the pool area. He found two chairs for us and sat me down next to one of his friends.

"Beck, this is DJ," he introduced me. I noticed DJ was reading a horoscope book.

"What are you reading?" I asked him, genuinely interested.

"My girl's a horoscope nut, a Capricorn, and she wanted me to read up on it," DJ answered. I just happened to be a Capricorn too.

"What sign are you born under, Johnny?" I asked.

"Aries, April 15", he answered.

"Oh no," I muttered in disbelief.

"Why, what's the matter with that?"

Suddenly I became very serious. "We're just not compatible, that's all."

He laughed and winked at me. "Well, we'll have to rewrite that book then, won't we Hon?"

He then took the book from DJ and studied it for a while. I thought it was very sweet that he at least tried to be interested.

Our pool time was cut short because there was a public relations function scheduled for all the men. Before we left, Slim took a picture of Johnny and me as we raised our screwdrivers in a toast. I was in seventh heaven. This photo would be forever etched in my mind. It captured the moment when we were together and everything seemed to be ahead of us.

All the Eagles left the hotel in the early evening. All of them except Mike, that is. He had a slight "problem" and he seemed to think that I could help him. He had met a girl at the show the day before and had a date lined up with her. The problem was that he had forgotten her name.

"Beck, you've got to help me. How can I fire on her if I don't even know her name?" For some reason, I told him I'd try to help.

First I told him it was none of my business but I suggested that he better not act as though sex was the only thing on his mind. Women don't like that, I explained. I thought he would have learned that by now.

A few minutes later she arrived. She seemed nice. Mike pulled out a chair for her at our table. He then started to introduce us.

"This is Becky, my buddy's girl."

I leaned forward. "What did you say your name was?" I asked her innocently, knowing full well that I was an accomplice. I was a betrayer of my own gender.

"I'm Debbie," she answered. She did not suspect a thing.

Mike winked at me. He put his arm around her back and gave her a side hug. They left the table and went into the bar. I then went back upstairs to wait for Johnny. When he arrived hours later, I could tell he had been drinking. We went back down to the bar together where most of the other guys were a little drunk too. Johnny made a point of telling me under his breath how good he thought he and I were getting along, especially in bed. I couldn't help but agree.

Just then Mike walked into the bar and when he saw us he rushed over to our table. "I did it, I nailed her, how about that!" he exclaimed.

You've sure got a lot of class, Mike, I thought to myself.

"Gosh Becky," he said to me, "You're okay for a hammer! You told me just how to play it and it worked. Good on you. I owe you one for sure."

I was now mortified that I had a hand in this. I felt sorry for Debbie, knowing she meant nothing to Mike. I sure hoped he meant nothing to her. I hoped she wasn't expecting anything more than a one-night stand.

Mike turned to Johnny. "Hey Johnny, you're pretty drunk. Don't you go and do anything stupid like asking Becky to marry you." He nodded in my direction. I blushed a little at his comment but Johnny didn't flinch. I wondered if Mike was seeing that his friend and I were clicking on all cylinders. I wondered if he could tell that I was becoming more than just another hammer.

Shortly thereafter we said goodnight to Mike and went up to our room. We couldn't wait to get into bed. I was so happy that our lovemaking was so important to both of us. We couldn't get enough of each other. Afterwards we just lay together quietly. I found myself wanting to share my feelings with him.

Hesitantly, I opened up to him. "Is this

possible, I mean, can this even happen in one day? I think I might be falling in love with you, Johnny. I don't quite believe it myself."

The whisper inside was telling me to stop talking but I pushed it away.

Johnny looked over at me and smiled. "Promise me, no bull, okay?" he said. "No lies, no games..." Then he added, whispering seductively, "Never. Not between us."

I hugged him close and made a promise I fully expected to keep.

"I want to see you again," he said, changing the subject. "We'll be at Clarksville, Tennessee in a couple of weeks. I'll send an Eagle escort for you if you can make it."

Wow! I thought. Clarksville is only an hour away from Nashville! How perfect!

"You know I'll be there, Honey, if I have to walk," I answered, hugging him as tightly as I could.

Just then the phone rang. You see what I mean about phones. It was Mike asking if the coast was clear.

"Sure, come on up, Mike. Okay Beck?" he asked me, not waiting for an answer. What could I say? After all, it was Mike and Johnny's room, not mine. Just like before, Mike entered the room, seemingly oblivious to us. He stripped down to his shorts and went right to bed.

I asked Johnny if it was okay for me to go to the airport with him in the morning.

"Of course you can go," he answered, "I want you to." I was realizing that this would be the last night I would be able to hold him for a while. I opened my eyes to look at him and was surprised to see him wide-awake, staring right back at me.

"What's the matter?" I asked softly.

"Nothing," he whispered. "Only that I've just got you for a little while longer and I don't want to waste a minute of it." He touched the side of my face. "Thank goodness you stayed." I filed this moment away as one of my sweetest memories.

"Go to sleep, silly," I said softly as I watched him until his eyes closed.

Morning came early. Neither of the guys had bothered to pack the night before so they were crazy busy. Everything had to be picked up and thrown into suitcases. I noticed how Mike and Johnny got along very well. They kidded with each other constantly. Despite my rough first impression, I was starting to like Mike. His dry sense of humor kept me laughing almost constantly.

Just when I thought we were all ready to leave, Johnny surprised me again. "I want you alone," he whispered hotly into my ear. He glanced over at Mike, winking. "Tell the crew chief I'll be running a little late today."

"I'm not tellin' nobody nothin'," Mike laughed as he shut the door behind him.

Johnny wanted to make love to me every chance we got. I felt the same way. It just seemed like we belonged together. I was overwhelmed by my feelings and I was sure that I loved him.

We waited until the last possible moment to leave. By the time we got to the airport, most of the ground crew was scurrying around getting ready for takeoff. I spotted Mike across the way talking to Debbie, the girl he'd been with the night before. I was relieved to see that they were still together.

"There's Mike," I told Johnny, putting my hand on his shoulder.

"Yup, there's my man," he answered. She's not a bad-looking hammer either. I've seen him with a lot worse."

"What's the story with Mike?" I asked. "Is he married? Where's he from?"

Johnny answered, "He's from Charlotte. Yes, he's married, but separated. His wife doesn't like all the partying and the traveling. I hope he can work things out. I'd hate to see him lose his family. He's got a couple of kids and he's lonely as hell out here on the road. That's why there's a different hammer every night. Marriage and this life, well they just don't mix. I told you that's why I'm not married."

This shed a new light on Mike. He was just a normal person after all. I found myself hoping that he could work everything out with his family.

We walked around for a little while. There must have been 500 people there waiting to watch the team take off. I wanted to hold hands with Johnny, something, just to touch him. He sensed it and he said so.

"I can't hold you the way I want to," he explained. "They're very strict with us about having hammers around the flight line. You can stay, but there can't be any public display of affection."

"Can't you even kiss me goodbye?"

"Well sure, but we have to play it cool."

Paul was there. We walked by him and everyone nodded and said hello. It was the first time I had seen him since the day we shared his hotel room in Pittsburgh. I felt as if the whole experience with him had never even happened and that I had been with Johnny all along.

Just then a blast of dust came out of

nowhere from one of the private airplanes that was taking off. Johnny spun me around and shielded me with his whole body. He then checked me over, wanting to know if I was okay. Other than a little dust under my contacts, I told him I was fine. I found it so endearing that he wanted to take care of me. A protective man is hard to resist.

All too soon the ten aircraft were ready to leave and I realized it would be only minutes before the ground crew would have to leave too. These last moments were precious. The jets filed out onto the runway and took off in a blazing display of glory. Everyone held their breath. What a beautiful sight! No matter how many times I would come to witness that take off, it would be just like the first time. I was totally awestruck.

The support plane started to wind up. Those on the ground crew were all running to climb aboard and before I knew it, Johnny had kissed me goodbye and was hurrying away.

"Oh please, don't go; don't leave me," I said in a voice that no one could hear. Yet it was as if he heard me, for he turned around and smiled.

"Two weeks baby!" he called out to me. I was too choked up to speak. I blew him a kiss

—

as he climbed into the plane. He waved to me a split second before the door closed and stole him from my view. The plane then taxied down the runway and took off. Just like that, he was gone. I looked around me. I didn't realize how many women were standing there with me. Most of them were crying.

All of a sudden, elation swarmed over me. I would be seeing Johnny in two weeks! Just fourteen days! I smiled at the plane, now a tiny dot in the sky. This was something I would never get used to, this saying goodbye, but this time I realized there was no need for me to feel sad. It is not goodbye!

I was already missing him as I slowly walked to my car and drove to the other side of the airfield to catch my flight home.

7
Air show: Clarksville

Back at work at the Nashville Airport, the girls couldn't wait to hear about everything that happened. When I told them that I'd met someone else and didn't end up staying with Paul after all, they were a little shocked. I didn't offer many details and they seemed to know enough not to ask too many questions.

It just so happened that it was time to choose our upcoming work schedules. Because the air shows had fast become my priority, I needed a schedule with most weekends off. I was lucky to have enough seniority to get what I wanted.

Later that day when things settled down, I found myself reliving every moment of the trip. I spent hours trying to dissect and analyze every word and every action, looking for the hidden meaning behind everything. Did Johnny really care about me? I desperately wanted to believe so.

As the time for the next show drew near, I couldn't understand why he hadn't called me. Because I did not yet understand the amount of time the Silver Eagles spent traveling, I couldn't help but take it personally. By the time Wednesday rolled around, I was getting anxious. The show was in just three days! Maybe he lost my number, I reasoned. Deciding to take matters into my own hands, I called the office directly. My hands were shaking as I dialed the main number to The Silver Eagle compound in Phoenix. Before I knew it, the operator had connected me and a voice boomed over the line.

"Silver Eagles, Specialist Thomas!"

I asked for Specialist Munroe and waited. What seemed like an eternity went by. Finally Johnny's voice was on the line.

"Specialist Munroe, how may I help you?" He sounded so polite.

"Hi, Johnny, this is Becky."

He didn't miss a beat. "Hi there. How are you anyways? We just got home last night. I was going to call you today. Are you still coming to Clarksville?"

All the anxiety from the last two weeks melted away. He wanted me to meet him in Clarksville after all!

"I sure am," I told him happily. "I've arranged for the time off."

"Good on you, Hon." he answered. He told me where they would be staying. I mentioned to him that Donna wanted to come along too. She had called me at least three times.

"Sure, bring her along. There are more than enough guys to go around, you know that," he laughed.

"Will Joe be there?" I inquired. Joe was the fellow Donna had been with in Nashville.

"Yeah..." Johnny replied, "He's on this trip, but I don't think he wants to be with her. Can you bring some of the other girls you work with?"

"Yes, maybe. I've told them all about it. There might be a few of them arriving Saturday," I replied.

"Okay, good. See you at the motel. Be careful driving!"

Friday seemed to drag by but I finally got out of work and picked up Donna. We were both anxious to get on the road so we could get to Clarksville before dark. We were running a little late and I thought I'd better call Johnny, thinking he might be worried. Sure enough, he answered the phone on the first ring.

"Where are you? I was just going to call your house. I was worried sick you had an accident or something."

"I'll be there in about fifteen minutes," I

reassured him. I was so excited I could hardly talk.

"Don't worry about anything, Honey. Hey, I've got two beds. Which one do you want?" I realized that he was teasing me and I could feel a swell of emotion rising up in my chest. I couldn't wait to see him. I couldn't wait to hold him.

"Wherever you're sleeping is fine with me," I answered softly, seeing him smile in my head.

We finally arrived at the motel. He had given me his room number but I couldn't find it. I could hear voices coming from the upper level. I listened for Silver Eagle lingo and sure enough, I heard Johnny's voice. As I got closer, I could hear him clearly. He was sharing the news with the other guys. "I've got a hole card coming in very soon. She's got one hammer with her and others are coming tomorrow. Hole cards? Hammers? More of that secret language. I knew what a hammer was. What was a hole card? I made a mental note to ask Johnny.

I followed the sound of their voices...and there he was, dressed in Bermuda shorts and looking absolutely adorable. He spotted me right away and within seconds he had his arms around me and lifted me off the ground so fast that I didn't know what happened. I was laughing and crying at the same time.

He had a single room this time because Mike wasn't on this trip. We couldn't get there fast enough. The door was barely shut when he pressed his body close to mine. He kissed me like he hadn't seen me in years. Then ...the phone rang. It was Donna. She was upset because I wasn't trying to find her a date. She told me she was heading back to Nashville. I didn't care. I hung up the phone and ran straight back into Johnny's arms. When I asked him if he had thought of me while we were apart, his answer was yes; that he had known it would be like this.

It didn't seem possible that the sex could be better than the last time, but it was. His touch ignited a passion in me that I had never felt before. I whispered that it was hard to believe that it had only been two weeks since we had seen each other.

"Two weeks is too long," he whispered back to me.

We seemed to intuitively know what the other wanted and needed. I was swept up in the emotion and the raw passion we felt for each other. At one point Karen Carpenter was singing "We've Only Just Begun" on the radio in the background and it was perfectly timed, just for us.

I would have been happy to stay right there with him in bed but the rest of the team would be arriving soon. It was important to Johnny that we be downstairs to greet them. We were laughing together as we left the room and we walked into the bar area holding hands. We were both deliriously happy.

It was like Old Home Week. Almost all the boys remembered me from Pittsburgh. I heard some fellas on my right ask who I was. Johnny heard them too and raised his chin, stating proudly, "She's my hole card." There, my question was answered. I hoped this was a compliment.

We had a few more drinks and then we went out to dinner. I tried to get him to talk about himself but he wouldn't elaborate much except to say he was a country boy from a small town in Georgia. His favorite dessert was Georgia peach pie with ice cream. Merle Haggard was his favorite singer. I was glad he liked country music, because I had always wanted to be a country singer. He smiled and told me I was definitely pretty enough. Smiling, I said, "I guess it should depend more on whether or not I can sing, not how I look."

He laughed. "It doesn't hurt to be good-looking too."

I leaned over and kissed him. I loved it when he said such sweet things like that to me.

Turning the conversation to a more serious note, I asked him how come he had never married. I couldn't understand that. I always thought the first thing you did when you went out on your own was settle down and have a family. Since he wasn't asking me anything about myself, I was relieved that I did not need to tell him about my failed marriage with Danny.

"Only once did I ever think about it," Johnny replied, "but then I joined the Eagles and I won't get married now. Like I said, this job and marriage don't go together. Not in my opinion. Maybe I'll think differently about it in a couple years."

When he asked me about my life, I explained I was just a simple Tennessee girl who loved country music and was happy to be living in the heart of it all, living in the heart of Nashville. He never asked me whether I was married or anything.

After dinner we had a drink at the bar. Kidding around, I teased him as I pondered aloud which Eagle I'd go out with next if he and I didn't work out. After all, the episode with Paul was still somewhat fresh in my mind. Johnny took me by complete surprise as he spun my chair around in one swift move and brought us face to face.

"Oh no, Honey, you're one man's hole card now, okay?" He was dead serious and I knew it. My heart skipped a beat as I felt the power of his words.

When we got back to the motel bar a little later, all the guys were there and everyone had been drinking for a while.

"Just think," Johnny told me, "if it weren't for the Silver Eagles, I'd have never met you." I smiled and told him that some things were just meant to be. As we got up to leave a little before closing time, he leaned in close to me.

"Give the guys the thumbs-up sign when we go out the door, okay?" he whispered in my ear.

"Sure, why not?" I turned around and did as he asked. I didn't realize this at the time but it was clear that Johnny was just showing off in front of the guys. He wanted them to know he had me. It was true. He did. He had me.

When we made love that night, I noticed a change in him. He was obsessed with pleasing me. The more I cried out and begged for more, the better he liked it. I told him over

---

and over what a marvelous lover he was, and I meant it. I loved to run my hands all over his body and feel the tremor of his excitement building to a fantastic release. All I cared about was having his body close to mine. We fit together like hand in glove.

8
The Next Day: Clarksville

The next morning he opened the door of our room and hollered out to the busload of Silver Eagles parked outside, "I'll be there in a few!" They responded with hoots and yells. He loved every minute of it.

My girlfriends from work were due to arrive around noon. The air show was scheduled for two o'clock so I told Johnny we would all see him at the show. With a big smile on his face, he kissed me and walked out the door. He always kissed me goodbye. I loved that.

It was not long after that, Emily and Patti arrived.

"Let's get on over to the show so we can see the guys before they get too busy," I suggested.

I was excited to show them every wonderful thing. Johnny had given me a Silver Eagle car card, which enabled us to drive right out onto the ramp. There must have been sixty thousand people there! I spotted Johnny's friend Steve in the crowd and called over to him to join us. I introduced him to

Emily and Patti. He couldn't take his eyes off Emily. He whispered to me, "That's the one I want, the little one."

"You do your firin' yourself," I answered, laughing. "You're a big boy."

There was an intense excitement in the air. Everyone was on the edge of their seats waiting for the Silver Eagles to perform.

I spotted Johnny coming towards us. How he found the car in the crowd was beyond me, but he confidently got into the driver's seat and I introduced him to the girls. Then he drove us right up beside the support plane so that we could see the show without any of the crowd standing in the way. He wanted us to have the very best seats in the house.

The throng of spectators cheered as the silver and blue jets taxied down the runway and took off. There wasn't a cloud in the sky to hinder the performance. It was a beautiful show. I sat there, spellbound the whole time.

After the show, the crowd was invited to come forward onto the ramp to get autographs. Emily and Patti went over to each of the pilots and had them sign their Silver Eagle brochures. I noticed Patti talking and smiling at great length with one of them. I watched as a couple of youngsters walked up to the members of the ground crew.

"Which airplane do you fly Mister?" one of them asked the crewman, handing over his brochure for an autograph.

"I'm on the ground crew, son," the man answered, smiling.

"Oh, never mind," the boy replied as he grabbed back his brochure. It was evident he was only interested in the pilots. I was a little annoyed as I was finding myself feeling very protective of the guys. I wanted to stick up for all the men that were part of the ground crew. I understood the dedication and how hard everyone worked to make these shows possible.

Emily, Patti and I headed back to the motel to wait for the guys to finish their workday. There was a public relations dinner scheduled for the men that night. As soon as they returned from work they changed clothes and we all went down to the bar. We had just settled in when I looked up and saw two more of our girls from Nashville out in the lobby. Without thinking, I yelled out to the group.

"Okay boys! Here come the hammers!"

All the guys laughed and I wondered how in hell I'd ever had enough nerve to say that. Being with Johnny had unleashed a braver and wilder side of me. It seemed my priorities were with the Silver Eagles now.

Johnny quietly suggested that all us girls go out to have a nice meal and then meet back later at the motel. This sounded like a great plan to all of us, so off we went. You can imagine the conversation around our dinner table!

The men's dinner was still in progress in the restaurant when we got back to the motel. We all quietly filed into the adjoining bar. Within what seemed like thirty seconds, Johnny was right there beside me. He was not going to let anyone else fire on me that was for sure.

We sat at a big table in the middle of the room. When dinner was over, one by one the group started to trickle in. Some of them were paired up; some of them were not. Johnny took it upon himself to make sure everyone had a partner. He grinned at me when he sat back down as if to say, "See? Nothin' to it!" I couldn't help but smile at the way he just took over and matched everybody up like that.

We sat there like two mother hens watching everyone have a good time. After a while he looked over at me and said softly, "You're the most beautiful woman in this room you know."

"You're a little biased," I whispered as I

leaned over to touch his face and tenderly kiss him. I loved this man.

He squeezed my hand. "You know," he said, "it's nice knowing we're going to be together tonight. No bull like the other ones around this table. We know that when it's time to leave, we'll be together and that's all that matters."

I noticed how he kept watching me intently. For a quick moment, I even dared to think that maybe he was falling in love with me.

Emily leaned over at one point and whispered in my ear. "He's only got eyes for you, kid. I noticed him at the air show. He hasn't even looked at another girl. You can sure tell you're not a one night-stand as far as he's concerned."

Those words meant so much to me. I whispered back, "Thank you Emily Davis. You have no idea how much I needed to hear that." Emily always seemed to know the right thing to say.

Everyone was having such a good time. I knew, unless I was badly mistaken, that most of the girls would be staying the night. The bar was crammed with people. Pretty girls were all over the place. Word must have gotten out in this small town that the Silver Eagles were staying here.

Johnny and I couldn't have been more pleased that everyone was having such a good time. We eventually slipped away for a quiet drink together and then went upstairs. We just wanted to be alone. As he unlocked the door, the phone was ringing. Of all people, it was Donna. Again. I was surprised to learn that she was back in the motel shacked up with Ralph, one of the crew chiefs. I guess she had come to realize that she could not stay away from the Silver Eagles. I kept looking at Johnny and got off the phone as quickly as I could.

There were no words spoken as we undressed each other. We had just made it to the bed when the phone rang again. This time it was Betty and she wanted to know where everybody was. I tried to explain that I couldn't help her. We had come upstairs and weren't paying much attention to anyone else. All I wanted to do was get back to Johnny. It's all I cared about. We reached for each other again with a passion that was beyond words. Then, wouldn't you know, the damn phone rang again! This time Johnny grabbed it off the hook.

"WHAT!" He bellowed into the receiver, "What the hell do you want?" The surprised look that came upon his face was pure panic when he realized who the caller was and what he had said. If he had a tail, it would've been between his legs.

"Yes, sir, Chief, she's here. Just a minute."

Johnny handed me the phone. It was Chief McGraw. He put Patti on the line with me. She wanted me to know that she was going home. I told her I was glad she came to see the show and wished her a safe trip home. It seemed that we were finally finished with all the phone calls. We took the phone off the hook and, just to be sure, we threw a pillow over it. Problem solved.

The men's work call came all too early the next morning. Johnny kissed me goodbye. He said he would be back in a couple of hours to get me. He was back in half an hour. As I finished getting dressed, he gave me a rundown of who stayed with whom the night before. Getting a hammer to stay with you was a status symbol. These men were bonded like brothers, but that didn't stop the teasing that went on all the time, especially when there were women around.

I went over to sit on the bed next to Johnny. In all the excitement I had forgotten to tell him that I could arrange to be with him that very same night in Indianapolis!

"Honey," I said, looking at him eagerly, "How would you like a hole card in Indianapolis tonight?"

"Are you kidding?" His eyes were wide with surprise. "Can you come up there?" He seemed pleased.

"Yep. There's a flight at five o'clock." I answered, trying to gauge his thoughts. Did he want me there? He seemed to be okay with it as far as I could tell.

"Are you sure you want me to come?" I asked.

"I would tell you if I didn't," he said rather abruptly. "Would you understand though, if I had another hole card up there?"

I hesitated for a moment, blinded by the thought of it.

"I would understand," I said quietly, "but I sure wouldn't like it."

He laughed and gave me a big hug.

I told him that I understood but I really didn't. It was a tough pill to swallow knowing he was sleeping around with other women when he wasn't sleeping with me. Nonetheless, I kept trying to convince myself that I was special to him.

We drove out to the airport in silence. He held my hand the whole time. I knew in my heart I should have told him the truth about how I felt. I should have been honest with him. I would come to realize one day that my remaining silent was a huge mistake.

All the girls must have gone home because no one else was around at the airstrip. Apparently no one cared enough to see them off this time. No one cared but me.

It was obvious now that I was an unusual twist to the hole card-thing. Because of show schedules and extensive traveling, real relationships were very hard for the men to come by because typically they were long gone the morning after the show. My flying privileges and flexible work schedule made it possible for me to see Johnny on a fairly regular basis. It gave us a better chance to get to know each other. It made me feel that this was one Silver Eagle who could actually have a relationship that could work out for the long term. It made me feel that it would be me.

We didn't have much time together before take off. The fellows all waved as they got into the support plane and all too soon Johnny kissed me goodbye. In an instant, he was out of the car and out of my reach.

"See you tonight," he called to me as he walked away. Once again he was gone, but the pain was momentary for it would not be long at all. I would be seeing him in Indianapolis in just a few hours.

I watched the planes take off. This time I stood by myself, smiling as I saw them disappear into the deep blue sky.

9
Air Show: Indianapolis

I only lived an hour from Clarksville, but by the time I got home it was midafternoon. I had to hurry to get ready to catch the flight to Indianapolis. The other girls who'd been to Clarksville were already back at work, so when I arrived at the airport I half expected to see "Love those Silver Eagles!" lettered all over the ticket counter. Everyone agreed that they'd had a great time. I teased Patti about her date.

"A jock, big deal," I said kiddingly.

"No, Beck," she answered, "He's not stuck on himself or anything. He's a real nice guy."

Emily was the one who was quiet this time. She must have fallen for Steve.

I managed to get the last seat on the plane to Indianapolis. We landed right on schedule. The first thing I did was call Johnny's motel. He was not in his room. I got a panicky feeling in my stomach. About a half hour later I tried again. Still no answer. Where was he? I found my way to the bus counter and within minutes I was on my way to his motel. I was more than a little nervous.

When I arrived, the girl at the front desk gave me the message that Johnny would be back in about an hour. For some reason I thought this meant he didn't want to see me. Why would I even think that? I was beginning to feel desperate. Just then, a blue maintenance truck came speeding down the driveway. As it came into view I could see Joe at the wheel and Johnny beside him, grinning from ear-to-ear. They stopped nearby and as he leapt from the truck, I called out to him.

"Hey, don't I know you from someplace?" I couldn't stop smiling. He grabbed the bag out of my hand.

"Why didn't you call? I didn't think you were coming."

I had worried for nothing. Just being with him again helped me to relax and realize that everything was okay. I took the blame. The mix-up had been my fault because I hadn't left a message for him when I called.

Their work was done for the day and the air show had been a huge success. Everyone was so tired from the swinging time at Clarksville the night before; we decided to make it a health night. No drinking or anything.

"Hello health," Johnny said as he

squeezed me and pulled me close.

After dinner we went to our room and watched TV. It would be an early night. It didn't matter to me. After all, I had flown to Indianapolis just to be near him so I couldn't have been happier.

As I was awakened by the morning sunlight peeking through the drapes, I reached out to him. He stirred and I kissed his face, his neck and his shoulders and rubbed his back. Once he was awake enough to realize what was going on, there was no stopping him.

"Whew!" he exclaimed afterwards, "I didn't think I had it in me."

"Why not?" I teased him. "You're not an old man."

"Sometimes I sure feel like it, Hon," he answered, smiling.

Bus call came early and he had to head out all too soon. I thought it was very thoughtful of him to arrange for Joe to pick me up and take me to the show site. Because of this, I was able to take my time getting ready and I felt really good about myself as we headed over to the show. As soon as we arrived at the flight line, Johnny came right over to the truck.

"Nice looking truck you've got here,

—

69

Joe," he said, as he looked the vehicle over seductively from bumper to bumper. They smiled and I realized that he was referring to me.

We had a little time until Johnny had to catch his flight, so he escorted me to the nearby coffee shop for breakfast. There were a lot of girls sitting around at the tables. Word must've leaked out that the Silver Eagles were in town.

Johnny approached a table of uniformed men and asked one of the mechanics if he would run me over to the other side of the airfield after he left so that I could catch my plane home. It comforted me to think that he wanted to be sure I was taken care of.

After breakfast we sat together in one of the maintenance trucks as we waited for his flight. Once again, these last moments were precious.

"I'm getting used to this," I blurted out without thinking. As soon as the words were spoken, I wished I could have taken them back. The whispers told me to be still. Johnny had a funny look on his face and I knew he was uncomfortable with my comment. Hole cards weren't supposed to be involved quite this way.

A blast of thunder and fuel interrupted

the tense moment and diverted our attention. We witnessed the aircraft file out onto the runway and take off in their usual diamond formation. The ten planes then made a final pass over the field. The crowd was cheering. It seemed like a goodbye salute, the perfect prelude to the goodbye I was preparing to say to him. With only a few minutes left before he had to leave, he started to tell me about his hometown class reunion, which would be taking place in a few weeks. He wanted very much to go. Unfortunately the team was bound for shows in California and he wouldn't have a moment of time to book plane reservations. I jumped at the opportunity to help him.

"Johnny, I can help you with this. Don't forget, I work for the airlines."

"Hey, could you? That would be wonderful," he answered. "Then I won't have to worry about it."

I copied down all his information on the back of one of the publicity folders and I promised I'd call him. He was pleased as punch that I cared enough to help him and that he would be able to attend the reunion after all.

Just then Joe ran over to our truck, waving his hands and yelling.

"Come on Johnny, let's go!"

The propellers had already started to revolve. Johnny bounded out of the truck enthusiastically. Panic struck me again.

"Johnny," I whispered through the open window, "don't forget me."

"I won't," he answered. "Keep your hands cold!" It was a joke between us that my hands were always cold, except when he was around.

As I watched him walk away, a memory surfaced. My dearly departed aunt, when she was a young woman, was to be married as soon as her devoted fiancé arrived from Europe. He died tragically the night before his flight when his cab was sideswiped on the way to the airport in Rome and rolled over. It was a horrible accident and he was killed instantly. She never recovered from the loss. She always felt that it was her fault because he was on his way to be with her. Ultimately I believed she died of a broken heart. The fear that something like that could happen to Johnny was always lodged in the back of my mind. That's what happens when you love this way and when you know that life can change in an instant.

He was the last one to jump on board. The support plane door slammed shut on his charming smile and within seconds the clumsy plane rumbled onto the runway. All too soon it lifted off the ground. I glanced around as I got out of the truck. There were no other women or spectators around. Completely alone on the vast airfield, I watched the plane until it became the smallest of specks and then disappeared into the great blue sky. The sad lyrics from a popular country song, "Silver Wings," echoed in my mind. My tears were flowing freely just as the appointed maintenance vehicle pulled up alongside me.

"Come on, Missy. I'll take you over to the terminal," the driver said gently. He seemed to understand. After all, this was probably not the first time he had come upon a woman in tears at the flight line. As I regained control of myself, I climbed into his truck.

"Are you off to California with the Silver Eagles?" he wanted to know.

"No sir," I answered softly. "I'm afraid not."

Despite my heartache, I somehow had the presence of mind to thank him for the ride as he dropped me off at the terminal building. With an hour to kill before my departure, I browsed through the gift shop at the airport. I noticed a small rack of books over to one side. One of the titles was, "Someone's Thinking of You." It was a beautiful book with lots of room for photos and captions. Oh what a great idea! I would put the pictures of our road trip on the pages and then mail it to Johnny. It would be such a great souvenir for him of our shared memories. With the book tucked under my arm, I felt a bit brighter as I checked in for my flight to Nashville.

10
FLASHBACK: MIAMI

Our plane was delayed two hours because of an engine problem. Now that I was on the way, I just wanted get home. My time with Johnny was fresh in my mind, but it was difficult to focus on the fun that we had. All I could think about was how sad I felt when he left. I sat back in my seat, closed my eyes and remembered another time; another place when feeling sad and alone was part of my everyday life...

The summer day had started like any other in Miami: hot, humid, chance of severe thunderstorms. This particular morning, I noticed that my car was gone from the driveway and that my husband, Danny, was gone too. A note on the refrigerator read: "Gone to get baseball tickets, home later." Out of the corner of my eye, I noticed a key on the kitchen table. I wondered about that for a moment, and then just assumed it was a spare. I remembered a time when Danny would have asked me to go with him to get the tickets, for we did everything together back then. I longed for the closeness we once had but it was clear that our love was beginning to fade.

I was relieved when I looked out the kitchen window and saw my next-door neighbor in her front yard.

"Hey Sue!" I called out through the open window, "do you want to go to breakfast? Maybe do some shopping?"

Sue waved in agreement and motioned for me to get into her car. We then spent a few hours having breakfast and checking out some sales. We had become good friends in the year we had been neighbors.

I was surprised upon my return that Danny had not yet arrived home.

The afternoon came and went. By dinnertime, I didn't know whether to be mad at him or worried. It was nothing new. He had done this many times before, but he had always managed to call me to say that he'd be late. This time was different. There was no call. I had an uneasy feeling that hit me in the pit of my stomach. I called into my job and told them I was sick. I wanted to be home when he came back. When he still wasn't home by nine o'clock, I called a couple of his friends to ask if they had seen him. No one had. Things were getting worse by the moment.

I went to bed more angry than worried, assuming that he had stopped to have a few drinks on his way back from the ballpark. Typical. By the next morning I was going crazy. I made a pot of coffee and called Steve, one of Danny's friends. He knew I was upset, so he and another buddy came right over. We discussed strategy. We all agreed that we would have known by now if there had been an accident. We would have known if Danny was in the hospital. Where was he? How would I find him? There were no answers. As we finished up the last of the coffee, Steve and the guys left. I promised to call them as soon as I heard some news.

I had to do something. Anything. After agonizing, I decided to report my car stolen. It wasn't about the car. I hoped the authorities would help me to locate my husband. I had been told that it was too soon to file a missing person report.

There was no call, no word from Danny. Days went by. Sue was kind enough to drive me back and forth to work. I was frantic with worry. What had happened to him? Was he dead in a ditch somewhere? Had he been kidnapped? All kinds of thoughts were running through my mind. A whole week had passed and I couldn't stand just waiting. On the eighth morning without him as I was preparing to file a missing person report, there was a faint knock on my front door. I looked out to see a young woman around my age standing there. When I opened the door I expected to hear that she needed directions or perhaps help with her car. What she ultimately needed to tell me I would never forget as long as I live.

First she asked if I was Becky. When I replied that I was, she asked if she could come in for a minute. I had no idea who she was or what she wanted. She seemed harmless enough so I invited her in. You can imagine my shock when she said she came to talk to me about Danny. Her name was Karen. My world was spinning as she explained that Danny was her boyfriend and they wanted to get married. The only obstacle was me. Me. His wife. She was asking me to grant him a divorce so that they could get married! I could hardly speak. I couldn't think. I had been totally caught off guard.

When my voice came back and I could think more clearly, I asked her where he was and how long the affair had been going on. She replied that Danny was at her house when she left about an hour prior. They had been seeing each other for about three months. He knew she was coming to see me.

I knew that he wasn't man enough to tell me himself. He was a coward. He made her do his dirty work. She wanted me to know he thought I was beautiful and he didn't want to hurt me. "It's just that we are so very much in love," she said. I almost laughed in her face and I said the first thing that popped into my head.

"You can have him. I never want to see him again. Now, if you would, please get out of my house."

After she left, I called Steve and filled him in. He didn't seem too surprised when he heard the news. It made me think that they all must have known about Karen.

I proceeded to file the missing person report anyway. Perhaps I wanted revenge. I called the police who informed me that finding him would be very difficult. Now I had to make it about the missing car.

After all the calls had been made, I tried to process what was happening to me. What would I do now? It was all so sudden. I was in a state of shock and disbelief as I realized I had to sort out a new plan for my life. The only thing that was clear was that I could not afford to stay here, nor did I want to stay with reminders of Danny everywhere.

—

I finally called my parents in Nashville and explained what had happened. My mother, I knew, was holding her tongue from telling me, "I told you so." She was very kind. She told me to gather up my things and just come home.

First thing the next morning I called into work and told my boss I was leaving Miami. A short time later the police called to tell me my car had been found off the highway a few miles from our house. The keys were on the floor under a mat. An empty bottle of bourbon was under the passenger seat. They kindly offered to drive my car back to my house after they heard my husband was missing.

I remembered the key on the kitchen table. It was now clear to me that he never planned to return at all. I thought back to Karen sitting on my couch asking me to give my husband a divorce. Were they together now? Did he just ditch my car and run off with her? Somebody must have given him a ride. I didn't spend much more time thinking about it because I couldn't come up with any explanation. The police returned my car that evening.

The next day I packed up my things and went next door to say a tearful goodbye to Sue. It was quickly sinking in that my marriage was over. I took one last look around my home and drove out of the neighborhood I had come to know.

It was twelve hours to Nashville. It was a beautiful day and I actually enjoyed the drive. I was surprised there were so few tears. There was sadness and some regret, of course, but by the end of the trip I was feeling an overall sense of relief. My parents greeted me with open arms.

I was home. I was free.

11

Should We or Shouldn't We: Atlanta

The blaring announcement to board the flight to Nashville startled me. My eyes flew open and I sat bolt upright. I was confused for I thought I had just arrived in Nashville but I had been deep in a daydream. It had been a very long time since I had last thought of Danny and the life I once shared with him. Looking around the large gate area, the boarding had just begun. I was soon on board and heading home.

The first thing I did upon arriving in Nashville was to make Johnny's plane reservations for his reunion. I then proceeded to throw every spare moment into making the little book for him. When it was finally finished, I thought it was a real masterpiece. I was eager to mail it the next day so that he would have it when the team got home from California.

In our free time, Emily and I studied the Silver Eagle show schedule with a fine-toothed comb. The only time we didn't both have to work was when the Eagles were scheduled to be in Atlanta, which happened to be the same dates as Johnny's reunion weekend. Neither one of us intended to make the trip without an invitation...or did we? In the back of my mind, I could hear Johnny's voice telling me to be sure to inform him in advance before trying to meet up with him. Apparently surprise visits were not a good idea.

The day finally arrived. Johnny had directed me to call him in Chicago. I couldn't remember him telling me why he was in Chicago and there was no Chicago show on the schedule. I tried not to think about the possibility of there being a hole card there. My fingers were shaking as I dialed his motel.

"No Miss, the Silver Eagles have not checked in yet," was the operator's reply. "We do expect them momentarily." Now at least I knew the whole team was there. I left a message for Johnny with my phone number. A few minutes later, he called. I fought to keep my composure so he wouldn't realize how excited I was to talk to him. I don't know why I was trying to hide my feelings. Yes, he was fine, California was beautiful, no he hadn't gotten into much trouble, and yes he was glad he was going home. He asked me about the status of his plane reservations and was thrilled that I had been able to get him such good connections.

"Wow, thanks a lot Beck," he said. "I wanted to go to this reunion and now I can."

I then told him how much Emily wanted to go to Atlanta and while I desperately wanted to go too, I restrained myself for I had learned by now not to push myself on him. He said he'd let Steve know.

"It's up to him to ask her, not me," he replied. I could tell he didn't want to speak for his friend. He sounded like he wanted to get off the phone. I wondered if he was uneasy perhaps thinking I would ask about the Atlanta trip too. He told me he'd call me to let me know how he made out at the reunion. He didn't mention anything about Atlanta. My feelings were hurt, no question about it.

That night I couldn't sleep. All I could think about was the Atlanta show. If Johnny liked me as much as he said he did, why didn't he ask me to go? The possibility that he would want to spend the time with his family never entered my mind. I was sure there must be a hole card in Atlanta. The whisper inside me told me that I was right.

I had long since become used to the phone ringing in the middle of the night, so when Patti called me at four o'clock the next morning, my heart never even skipped a beat.

"Guess what!" she exclaimed. She didn't wait for an answer. She was practically screaming with excitement. "Larry just called me!"

"Larry who?" I questioned.

"Larry! Chief McGraw!"

I sat bolt upright in bed. Larry had called her? Well, how about that? What a lucky girl.

"He asked me to come to Atlanta. I can't go because of the days involved, but he asked me. That's the important thing. Becky, he asked me!"

So Larry had called and asked her to join him in Atlanta. I was happy for her but was feeling a bit sorry for myself. I wanted Johnny to ask me too. I missed him so much.

Emily and I had given up on the idea of showing up and surprising Johnny and Steve at the Atlanta show. We threw caution to the wind and decided we would call them at the last minute instead. We both knew it might not work out but we wanted to take the chance. In the meantime, we made alternate plans to go to Hilton Head where my parents owned a condo right on the beach. We caught the flight the next afternoon and by evening Emily and I were enjoying a beautiful coastal night. We tried not to think about Atlanta and the fact that we had not been invited.

The air show was Saturday. We waited until Friday evening to tell Johnny and Steve that we were coming. Emily sat next to me as I dialed the motel in Atlanta. She was still sitting next to me two hours later as I kept getting the same answer from the operator. "Nope, the Silver Eagles have not checked in yet but we are expecting them at any time now."

Finally about midnight Mike answered the phone in their room. He was surprised to hear my voice. "Hey Becky, where ARE you? I laughed to myself. I bet he thinks I'm right outside the door.

"I'm in South Carolina with Emily," I answered, "Where's Johnny?"

"He's out with his brothers and his mother. They came over from Athens. Can I have him call you when he gets in?"

I told Mike that Emily and I would be in Atlanta the following afternoon, as we would be making a stop there on our way home. I remembered telling Johnny that I would never lie to him. The only way to get to Nashville from Hilton Head was to change planes in Atlanta. This was, conveniently and honestly, the only connection we could make. Because there were no connecting flights out Friday night, we would have to stay in Atlanta overnight. Of course I planned it that way.

"Hey, that's great," Mike replied. "I'll tell him. He'll be glad to see you, you can bet on that." Mike was always on my side. As I hung up the phone, I hoped he was right. I sure hoped Johnny would be happy to see me.

I looked over at Emily. She was ecstatic. She knew that Steve would want to see her and hopefully Johnny would tell him that she was here with me. The whispers inside me were telling me not to go, but I wanted to see Johnny so much that I didn't listen to them. After all, it had been a whole month since we had been together and in my mind one month was far too long for us to be apart.

I called Mike again the next morning.

"Hmmm, Johnny must have stayed over with his family because he didn't come back last night," he told me. "Don't worry though, he'll be here soon and I'll tell him you're coming! See you later."

As I hung up the phone, Emily and I realized it was probably a good thing we had made a room reservation for ourselves, just in case.

The next day I said a silent prayer as we boarded the flight to Atlanta.

12
Air Show: Atlanta

We arrived in Atlanta, caught a cab and headed straight for the hotel. After we checked into our room, we just sat on the bed looking at each other. What on earth were we doing? It now all seemed ridiculous that we hadn't been invited and yet we came anyway.

There was a knock on the door. I opened it not knowing quite what to expect. It was Steve.

"I just took all my makeup off!" Emily screamed at him in jest.

"So what," he answered and next thing you know they were laughing and kissing. The first chance I got I asked him about Johnny.

"I'll try to find him for you," he answered.

"What!" I exclaimed. I didn't understand.

"Now don't go getting upset. Mike told him you were coming. He's with his family, that's all," he explained.

Then the phone rang. "This place is like Grand Central Station," I said as I grabbed up the receiver.

It was Mike. He wanted to tell me that Johnny knew I was here to see him. "He said he'd see you back at the hotel for sure," Mike reassured me. "He said to tell you that it's okay and not to worry, Becky."

"Thanks Mike, we're even now." I remembered when I helped him with that girl's name he had forgotten. Debbie.

I wondered why Mike always helped me. What was in it for him?

The phone rang again. This time Steve answered it.

"Yeah, she's here, what's it to you?"

It was Johnny.

He handed the phone to me. I calmly said hello.

"Hi Doll, when did you get here? Come on up. I'm in room 500. I've got to take my mother to dinner, but we can talk for a few minutes. Can you come?"

"Sure, be right there. I've got some time." There was no hesitation on my part.

"Steve, how do I look?" I asked.

"You look fine, hammer," he answered. "Now go on."

"Aw, shut up, you just want Emily alone," I laughed, as I went out the door.

I walked up the stairs trying to take

some deep breaths to calm myself before seeing Johnny again. When I knocked on the door, he answered immediately. There he was, grinning at me from ear to ear with shaving cream all over his face. How adorable he looked! I was so happy that he was so glad to see me! I had worried too much. I maintained my composure and smiled at him.

He explained what had happened the night before. "Mike told me you called last night but I stayed with my brother and didn't come back here. He told me you were coming." After wiping the shaving cream off his face, he walked over to me, wrapped his arms around me and kissed me hard. My heart was beating wildly. Against my better judgment I felt myself responding to him. His voice was husky again. "Do you have to leave right away?"

"No, why?" I answered.

"Because I want to make love to you--- now."

We undressed quickly. We had been apart for over a month. The excitement was too much. Our lovemaking was over too soon.

He kissed my face over and over. "I'm so glad you're here," he murmured. Of course, right on cue, the phone rang.

"I'm surprised it didn't ring five minutes ago," Johnny laughed.

It was Joe and he was on the way up. We hurried to get dressed. The look on Joe's face when he saw me was utter shock. It was obvious he never expected to see me there, that's for sure. He only stayed a moment and then he left. I wondered what that was about.

Johnny told me all about his reunion and how much he enjoyed himself. He thanked me again for making his plane reservations.

"Just think, if my family wasn't here we'd have it made," he said frowning, "but what can I do?"

"I understand," I said simply. "You didn't ask me to come. I'm on my own this time."

"I'll tell you what Becky, I'll call you when I'm on the way back tonight, OK? It will be late, probably one or two o'clock in the morning."

That was fine with me. He walked me back to my room and kissed me goodbye. As he left, I couldn't resist calling out to him that somebody had told me the Silver Eagles were in town.

"That's what I heard!" He was laughing as the elevator door closed behind him.

Emily and Steve had gone over to the club so I used the time alone to take a shower and set my hair. When they came back it was very late. Emily wanted to take a bath and relax, so Steve and I went down to the bar for a drink. In the lobby I ran right into Chief McGraw. He recognized me and I told him how much Patti had wanted to come but she simply couldn't get the time off. He nodded like he understood and walked away. He seemed a little uncomfortable talking to me. Maybe he's married, I thought. It was lonely in the bar without Johnny. I couldn't wait for him to come back.

We had to make some adjustments with the rooms so that Steve and Emily could be by themselves and I could be alone with Johnny when he got back. I was learning about "pulling slack." There was only one hitch. Johnny never came back.

By the next morning I was so upset I couldn't think straight. I never slept a wink all night. No matter what Steve and Emily said to me, I was inconsolable. Johnny had told me he would be back and I had waited for him. I could not believe that he would hurt me this way.

Mike came down from his room and the four of us went out to breakfast. I had changed my opinion of Mike in the months since I first met him. He had become a good friend to me. At breakfast I asked Mike to level with me.

"Okay, Becky," he started, "but I would rather not have to tell you this. It seems that Joe's family lives in Atlanta and Johnny had dated his sister in the past. This whole thing has been set up for months," he continued, "and Johnny couldn't do anything about it." I then remembered how surprised Joe was when he saw me in Johnny's room the day before.

"Johnny told me last night that he would try to get back to the hotel but he didn't see how he could. Don't be mad at him." Mike said gently, "He didn't ask you to come."

"I know, I know," I answered. "I'm not mad because he didn't come back. I'm mad because he lied to me. He told me right from the beginning, no lies."

"Well," Mike said, "forget about it today and let's go out to the club and have a good time." He squeezed my hand. Oh no, I thought, don't tell me Mike is firing on me. I was beginning to realize that any of them at any time would say or do whatever was necessary to get a girl into bed.

After the boys went to work, Emily and I sat in our room and talked. Finally the tears came. Johnny was no different than the rest of these guys and it was about time I realized it. I felt better after talking it through with her. We got dressed to go to the club with me swearing I would have a good time no matter what.

We called a cab and the driver had no idea where it was we were going. It was so ridiculous it was funny. We finally got to the club after taking all the wrong roads. We had laughed so hard that we were both in a good mood. I made believe I didn't care if I saw Johnny or not.

There were a lot of people in the club but Emily and I got great seats right by the door. I saw Joe coming in and kicked Emily under the table. He was with a girl about my age and an older woman we figured must be his mother.

Emily whispered, "That girl must be his sister, Johnny's hole card." We knew Joe would have stopped to say hello otherwise. His sister was very attractive and I realized quickly that knowing Johnny was with other women and actually seeing him with other women were two different things. I tried to cover so no one would see how upset I was.

We could tell the air show was over because the Silver Eagles started to trickle in. Steve and Mike were the first ones to come through the door.

Mike couldn't wait to tell me what Johnny did last night.

"Johnny stayed with Joe's sister last night. One of the other guys told me." Mike was such a gossip hound.

"So where is he now?" I asked.

Mike answered, "Over at the show site about thirty miles from here. He'll be here in a little while."

Emily and Steve went into the other room to have dinner. That left Mike and me alone at the table. Johnny finally arrived and came right over to us. He sat down right across from me.

"My man, Johnny, well, son of a gun," snickered Mike. "Where have you been?"

Johnny answered, "Down at the show site, Mike, and boy was it hot out there today." He was trying very hard to avoid looking at me.

Johnny asked Mike if he wanted a drink then glanced at me. "How about you Becky, are you ready?" He had finally acknowledged my presence at the table.

I nodded yes and when he went up to the bar, Mike whispered, "I'll leave as soon as he gets back."

As soon as Johnny sat down, Mike excused himself and headed for the men's room. I then leaned across the table and looked at the man I thought I was in love with.

"Did you think you could make love to me yesterday and then just walk out and forget about me?" I knew my eyes were blazing because I was so mad.

"I could make love to you right now," Johnny responded quietly. "There's no reason why this should spoil anything that you and I have." He continued, "I got drunk last night and stayed with my brother."

"You're lying, you bastard, I know you stayed with Joe's sister and as far as I'm concerned, we're through." My voice was calm and steady, which surprised the daylights out of me.

His wasn't though. "For God's sake, we're not married," he practically yelled.

"You're damn right we're not, Mister. Remember you said that!" I was surprised at the strength of my outburst.

This was the first time Johnny and I had any kind of argument or disagreement. It was very unusual for me to speak up like that. Mike returned and then without saying one word, Johnny abruptly got up and left the table. It was obvious how mad he was.

"How did you make out?" Mike asked.

"I don't know what to think, but the hell

with him," I answered.

Emily and Steve came back from dinner and I told them what had happened. Emily just laughed and said, "He wouldn't have gotten so upset if he didn't care." When she and I walked over to the ladies room a little while later, I saw Johnny at a table with Joe and his sister.

"I thought they left, Emily. They must've come back in. He looks like he's having a terrible time." The four of us, on the other hand, were having a great time. Mike was flirting with me and I was starting to think maybe I would stay with him. It seemed fair. Johnny was with his hole card, so why not?

The evening passed and it was time to call it a night. When we got back to the hotel, Mike called to see if Johnny was in their room. He and that girl were just leaving. I wondered why they were in his room. I listened to Mike answer a question from Johnny.

"You bet she's with me, so what?" Mike said.

"What did Johnny say?" I demanded when they hung up.

"Oh, some bull about having to sleep on the couch over at Joe's because his whole family is there. He asked again if you were with me, and when I said that you were, he called me 'a dirty bastard'."

I hesitated. I wondered if Johnny could be telling the truth after all. I decided right then to spend the night in my own room by myself. Mike understood when I explained my decision. I invited him into my room but only to talk. It was obvious that Mike wanted me to stay with him, but I couldn't bring myself to have sex with him just because Johnny might be with Joe's sister.

Mike swore up-and-down that Johnny would call me. He said that Johnny wouldn't be able to stand the thought of Mike being with me. Out of the blue he then asked me, "Hey, Becky would you let Johnny hang out with me if you and him got married?"

"What!" I said with surprise, "What are you talking about?"

He answered, "I just wondered, you know the way I am about running hammers."

"If I married Johnny," I answered softly, "I'd trust him completely and I'd never try to hold him down."

Mike sat down next to me on the bed and looked at me. "Boy, they sure don't make hammers like you every day. I've only met one other and she married somebody else." I asked Mike about his personal life without letting on what Johnny had told me. I tried to help him to see that it was important that he reconcile with his family. Mike said good night then and asked if I was sure I was okay by myself. I reassured him, kissed him on the cheek and shut the door behind him as he left. I lay down on the bed with my emotions all over the place. What the heck was Johnny doing? Was he really sleeping on the couch? Finally I was able to settle down enough to get a few hours of sleep.

The next morning the four of us headed for the airport. Mike asked me to call him later that night so he could share with me what Johnny said on the plane. "Don't worry about him, Becky, I'll take care of everything," he promised. "Just do me one favor okay? When he asks you to marry him, laugh at him." I smiled at Mike's joke but underneath I wondered if he knew something I didn't.

Emily kissed Steve goodbye. She realized this might be the last time she saw him. I hugged her. We all hated goodbyes. We boarded our flight praying we would make it back in time for work. We had cut it really close.

All the way back to Nashville, all I could think about was what Johnny would say when he confronted Mike on the plane. Would we break up over this?

13
Air Show: Dallas

Atlanta had been a nightmare. Five minutes of sex with Johnny didn't make up for everything else that happened. Of course all the girls back at work at the airport wanted to know the details. Emily and I wouldn't tell them anything. I went through the motions of work but my mind was already on the phone call to Mike that night. What did Johnny say to him on the plane on the way home?

Steve answered the phone when I finally made the call.

"Mike's right here, Becky, hang on a minute." I held my breath.

Mike took the phone. "Hey Beck, guess what? Johnny came right over to me on the plane all upset. He wanted to know if I had beaten him out for you. He wanted to be sure he hadn't lost you for a hole card. I told you he'd be upset. I told him you wanted to come to Dallas next week." I felt like I could breathe again for the first time in days.

"Hey, Becky are you there?"

"Yes I'm here," I answered. "It's just so

hard to believe."

"I told you, he digs you that's all. I knew everything would be all right. I know my man John."

"Well, Mike, it looks like I'll see you next week after all. Thanks a lot." I was so grateful to him.

Two days later I was in the middle of a real mess at work. A plane had been two hours late. Passengers were mad and it was very difficult to keep everything calm. The Silver Eagles were the furthest thing from my mind at the moment. I was patiently trying to explain to a very well dressed gentlemen that no, the planes were not late on purpose. Yes, we would call Chicago and give the message that he would be late. Yes sir, we'll be glad to give you a meal ticket. The phone rang on my desk.

"Gate 2, Becky speaking," I answered automatically. It was Richie in the operations office.

"Can you take a break and come in here for a minute? I've got something for you." Now what, I thought. What more could happen today?

"I'll be right there," I answered.

I excused myself from the onslaught of angry passengers and walked down the corridor to our flight operations office. I figured the boss probably wanted to keep me on overtime or something. I opened the door marked "Restricted Do Not Enter" and walked in.

"What's up?" I asked the harried man behind the desk.

"Phone call," he muttered without lifting his head. "Long distance. I thought it might be important." I studied the scrap of paper he had handed me: CALL JOHN IN COLORADO SPRINGS ASAP. The phone number was scrawled across the paper. I read it over and over. I was in shock. Johnny had called me! Mike had been right after all.

In a daze I walked out into the hallway. Johnny had called me all the way from Colorado Springs! I knew of a phone booth away from the mainstream of people where I was able to place the call. Johnny answered on the first ring and before I even had a chance to say hello, he invited me to go to Dallas the next week. Over and over he said, "We'll make up for Atlanta."

I explained that I would have to check on whether I could get the days off and I would call him back the first of the week. I had already asked for the time off but I sure was not going to let him know it!

"Try, Baby, try. Please," he said as he hung up. I was so happy! In seven days I would be in his arms again!

The next few days were spent duplicating the book I had made for him. The first book must have gotten lost in the mail. It was a lot of work but when it was finished it was just as funny and sincere as the first one. I'd give it to him in person this time.

When I called him the following week, he seemed thrilled that I could go and even promised to meet my flight at the airport. Something was different, but I wasn't about to complain.

I called a couple of friends who worked at the Dallas airport and asked them to meet me at the hotel the day of the air show. That way Johnny didn't have to worry about my transportation to and from the show when he was working.

The flight to Dallas the next day was right on schedule, thank goodness. I was so excited I don't think I would've been able to stand it if it had been even one minute late. Emily walked down to the gate with me at departure time.

"Have fun Becky," she whispered, "and try not to spend all your time in bed," she laughed. "Say hello to all the boys!" she called as she waved goodbye from the ramp. "Give them my best." We both realized that she wouldn't be on another trip this year. She and Steve had said their goodbyes in Atlanta. Her hole card days were over, at least for this year.

As excited as I was, I managed to relax on the plane and before I knew it, the stewardess was putting my seat tray up. "We're on final approach now," she smiled. I looked out the window at the skyline of Dallas. I had never been to Texas. Does everyone wear cowboy boots and cowboy hats?

I adjusted my make up and smoothed my hair. I hoped nothing had happened to delay Johnny. The wheels touched down; we heard the scream of the brakes and we were taxiing toward the terminal building. When the door opened, I deplaned slowly taking every precaution not to trip over my own feet. I knew he might be watching me and I wanted to make a somewhat elegant entrance for him to remember me by.

As I reached the foot of the stairs, I spotted Johnny coming towards me dressed in his Silver Eagle black dress suit. He kissed me right in front of everybody and looked deep into my eyes. I wanted to cry I was so happy.

We stopped to have a drink at the airport bar where he explained that he had to attend a work function back at the hotel. He would try not to be gone very long. Neither of us mentioned Atlanta, thank goodness. That nightmare had been forgotten, at least for now.

By the time we reached the hotel, it was late and I was concerned he'd be in trouble for being delayed. He appreciated my concern but told me there was no problem. After he made sure that I was comfortable, he got ready to leave. I walked him to the door and he reached for me. My whole body relaxed against him as he kissed me passionately.

"Wait for me. I'll be back as soon as I can."

"Honey, I'll be here," I smiled.

He blew me a kiss as he left the room. No one should be this happy, I said to myself as I turned on the TV and settled down to wait for him. I fully expected him to be gone at least two hours and I was happy and surprised when I heard the key in the door about half an hour later. He grinned as he opened the door and held his hand out for me to join him. Holding hands and smiling, we went downstairs for a few drinks.

As we walked into the bar the first person I recognized was DJ.

"Hi," I called out, "How's your Capricorn

sweetheart?"

"Fine," he said "just fine."

"Johnny Honey," I whispered, "just remember you and I aren't compatible."

"You and that damn book," he said as he squeezed my hand. "I told you we'd rewrite it."

We sat in a corner booth away from the crowd. He mentioned that he had dropped Mike's suitcase on his foot and it was bothering him a lot. I told him I'd help him forget the pain later. He smiled and hugged me. We were just talking back-and-forth when suddenly he took a hold of both my hands.

"Honey," he said seriously, "would you go with me if I wasn't a Silver Eagle?" I was surprised that he would ask such a question. He always seemed so sure of himself. Before I had a chance to answer, Mike and some other guys came in and clustered around us at the table. Johnny excused himself and went up to the bar to order a round of drinks. These were men I had not met before. Mike explained they were part of the parachute team that sometimes traveled on the same shows. One of them actually fired on me.

"Hey Baby, why don't you leave this Eagle guy you're with and come along with me? We'll go someplace nice and quiet so we can talk." I was so shocked I couldn't answer him but Mike spoke up for me.

"She's happy where she is. Just go on now and let her be."

The parachute guy just shrugged his shoulders, winked at me, and walked away. What a creep, I thought.

When Johnny returned, Mike told him what happened. I asked Johnny why that guy would even bother to fire on me knowing I was with him.

"You don't understand Dear," he explained patiently, "we all believe that if a guy can't hold his hammer, he doesn't deserve to have her. He just wanted to see if you were satisfied being with me."

"Let's go upstairs and I'll show you," I whispered.

"Wow, Babe, that's the best offer I've had this trip," he laughed.

"By the way, Johnny," I asked, thinking about the two parachute guys. "Would you ever jump out of an airplane?"

"Hell no," he answered, "It would have to be a damn good reason for me to even think about it."

Good, I thought, because it's way too dangerous. I'd be scared to death if he wanted to try that.

Everybody was trickling out by this time. Even Mike said goodnight and got ready to leave. Johnny told him to call in the morning before he came in to change his clothes.

"This is the last time I pull slack so you can be left alone Johnny, remember that." Mike winked at me as he walked out the door. I hadn't realized that Johnny and I would be alone for the night. There would be no one in the other bed to worry about.

We left the bar arm in arm and walked slowly upstairs to our room. All I could think about was giving him the book and wondering what his reaction would be. This would prove how he felt about me. A slight nervous twinge made its way into my stomach as we entered the room. Here goes, I thought.

"Honey, sit down and make believe you haven't seen me in a long time. Let's pretend that what I'm going to give you has come in the mail, okay?"

"Sure," he asked. "What is it?"

"I'll go change my clothes while you look at it."

He nodded his head agreeably. I handed him the book and disappeared into the bathroom. I could hardly unzip my dress. If he didn't appreciate the book, I might as well kiss him goodbye.

His laughter cut the silence like a rocket. It was music to my ears! I breathed a sigh of relief and opened the door. He was sitting on the bed laughing his head off. It was worth every minute of work, I thought, he really likes it!

" You don't think it's silly?" I asked as I sat down beside him.

"Silly, are you kidding? It's great! You must have gone through a lot to make this up. You're quite a hammer." I was beyond thrilled that he liked it and appreciated what I had done. Sitting there together, he reached for me and I melted into his arms. My whole world began and ended right there.

"All I want to do is please you," he said over and over. "I don't care about myself." I felt the same way. I just cared about making him happy. We made love for hours, both of us delighting in the moments that came so few and far between. Finally we were both exhausted.

"I love you," I whispered, "I swore I'd never say it again but I can't help it, I love you."

He smiled and kissed me. His eyes shone with happiness. Our relationship seemed to be deepening. All I wanted was to be close to him.

"This is what it means to be completely and utterly satisfied," he whispered...and we held each other as we drifted off to sleep.

14
The Next Day: Dallas

The morning alarm went off and Mike called two seconds later to see if the coast was clear. Johnny got up, unlocked the door and then headed straight for the shower.

Mike sauntered in as only Mike could do. I was lying there in bed with a sheet pulled up over me. This was not the first time. He knew I was embarrassed and he winked at me to put me at ease.

Just then Johnny came out of the bathroom with a towel wrapped around his waist. "Hey Mike, for God's sake, next time pack your suitcase a little lighter. My foot throbbed all night."

"Yeah, I bet it did," Mike answered as he looked over at me. I threw a pillow at him and we all had a chuckle over that.

As Johnny and Mike were getting ready to leave, Johnny asked me if one of my friends could drive me to the air show the next day. "I'm concerned about the driving," he said, "what if I get lost and miss my plane?"

"Don't worry Hon," I answered, "I've got it covered. My friend Marcy will take me." I was so glad I had the foresight to put the plan in place.

"Okay good. See you at the show then. I'll be at the trailer." He kissed me goodbye and left.

The girls showed up a little while later. They were old buddies of mine and were absolutely amazed at the closeness Johnny and I shared. Marcy couldn't wait to ask me how I could just stay with Johnny in his room. Wasn't I embarrassed? I told her no, everyone treated me with the utmost respect. I couldn't expect anyone else to understand this "arrangement" when I barely understood it myself. It was just the way things were on these trips. If you wanted to be a hole card, you had to learn to accept it for what it was.

"Come on, we'd better leave. Don't know how the traffic will be," I said. Well, just as I thought, the traffic was terrible. Everybody in the world must be going to the air show. Again we had been given a pass, which allowed us to pull up ahead of all the cars and park on the ramp. Being a hole card sure pays off in more ways than one I thought, as we got dirty looks from the less fortunate frustrated drivers.

We parked the car as close as we could to the flight line and headed for the public announcement trailer. There were upwards of

80,000 people in attendance waiting with great anticipation for the Silver Eagles to perform.

In their work uniforms, the men all looked alike to me and I had a tough time finding Johnny. There were police standing at the flight line restraining the crowd. As I walked toward the trailer, I spotted Paul coming toward me. Without realizing what I was doing, I started to walk right out onto the ramp. I called out to Paul and as he started to walk my way when a policeman grabbed me. "Hey, miss, you can't go through there."

Paul took the cop's hand off me. "Let her go," he said to the officer as he winked at me. "She can go out there, she's one of the Silver Eagles." The cop dropped his arm and let me through.

There we were, Paul and I standing in front of the crowd. I felt like a real ass. "What did you do that for?" I laughed, "I was just looking for Johnny."

"Well, he's not at the trailer. He must've gone over to one of the food tents." He smiled at me and walked away. I couldn't wait to fade back into the crowd. My friends thought the whole thing was extremely funny but I didn't. I walked in the direction of the food stands and spotted Johnny and Mike heading our way. I approached Johnny directly and nonchalantly asked, "Don't I know you from someplace?" We laughed easily and he asked me what the hell I was doing out there by the trailer. When I explained what happened, he shook his head.

"I don't understand how you get away with things. What a hammer."

Soon it was time for the show. As he left, Johnny gave me strict orders not to leave that spot. Once again the throng of spectator voices was replaced by the powerful hum of jet engines. Everyone held their breath as the United States Silver Eagles flew off into the sky. It was one of the best shows of the year. The weather was perfect. The show lasted about thirty-five minutes. All 80,000 people were justifiably thrilled beyond words. The applause was deafening as the pilots deplaned when the show was over.

Johnny came over as soon as he could and explained that he would be tied up for quite a while. We left then and went back to the hotel. The girls dropped me off and I headed for the pool. Now was a good time for a short nap. These trips drained my energy.

I didn't realize how long I had been by the pool; I had lost track of time. What was keeping everybody? Surely they must be through working by now. I went up to the room to wait. As usual I was worrying needlessly, for within just a few minutes they showed up. First came Johnny, then Mike and then Steve. Johnny asked me where I had been. Evidently he had been trying to call me for a couple of hours.

"I was down by the pool, why?" I wondered.

"I just wanted to tell you we'd be a little late that's all," he answered. I kissed him and told him how thoughtful he was. Mike snickered.

"Aww, shut up Mike," I said, "Mind your own business."

Johnny broke in before an argument started. "Come on you two, let's go downstairs and have a drink."

Silver Eagle uniforms were everywhere! Most of the guys had stopped for a drink as soon as they got back to the motel. Johnny and I sat at a table by ourselves. He took my hand and asked me seriously, "Are you happy when we're together?"

"You know I am," I said softly, "but I'd like to clear something up if it's okay."

"Sure, what's that?" Johnny asked. I took a deep breath and started in on what I knew would be a touchy subject.

"Is it all right with you if I look at the show schedule to see when I can meet you?" I paused, waiting to see his reaction. Slowly he nodded yes. I explained that I needed to request my flight passes ahead of time.

"You know I want you with me whenever we can make it happen," he answered. "Just be sure to let me know."

I relaxed a little. This conversation actually went better than I thought it would. He turned to face me.

"Hey, by the way," he asked, "Where did you stay that night in Atlanta?" Oh, how I was dreading this. My blood turned to ice.

"You know," I answered.

"If I knew, I wouldn't ask you. Where did you stay?" His gaze was steady and unwavering.

"In my own room." I stated, louder than was necessary. "Didn't Mike tell you on the plane?" I continued. "I did not stay with him. I thought about it and decided not to, even though I knew you were staying with Joe's sister."

"You believe what you want to there. You stayed by yourself in your own room?" Johnny asked.

"Yes," I replied. "Why? Would you have been mad if I had stayed with Mike?"

"No, I wouldn't be mad, only because I would know that Mike fired on you and not the other way around. All's fair in love and war."

I couldn't help it. My eyes filled with tears of relief. I had been very concerned about this and I wanted to be sure he understood that I hadn't slept with Mike.

"Aw come on, Hon, don't cry," he said as he cupped my face in his hands. "I want to tell you one more thing though." I looked up at him through my tears.

"You," whispered my romantic Silver Eagle, "are the greatest thing since peanut butter." Slowly a smile stole its way across my face. He always knew just the right thing to say.

We clung to each other in bed that night as if we both realized how close we had come to losing each other.

"We're an awful lot alike," Johnny whispered as he made love to me. Our lovemaking had reached new heights of joy. Every new experience added to our overall sense of happiness in pleasing each other. In my mind, this was what real love was all about.

"Let's rest for a while," he whispered, after a particularly good session. I snuggled up to him and we talked and laughed for what seemed like hours. The privacy was too good to last. There was the familiar knock on the door.

"Get lost, Mike!" Johnny called out, but he got up and let him in.

"Johnny, you listen to me," Mike said as he took his shirt off. "This is the only hammer I'll ever let stay in our room, remember that." He then said goodnight, got into his own bed, turned over and went to sleep. Johnny and I kissed and spent the rest of the night wrapped up together.

The next morning a magical sunrise was visible through the window. I felt that the sun was rising just for us. We both woke at the same time. Johnny touched my face and whispered, "Do you remember last night? That's the way it's supposed to be. It was just getting good when Mike walked in, wasn't it."

I kissed him good morning and told him that of course I remembered. How could I forget something so beautiful? I then gave him a little speech. You could tell by the look on his face how surprised he was when I talked that way. "Johnny, I'll never say I don't want you to sleep with any other hammers. I want you to sleep with all of them. Then if you still come back to me, you'll realize we have something very special. Last night proved that. I already know." He nodded in agreement but didn't say anything because the alarm went off and he had to get up to get dressed and fly away again. I wondered if he would think about what I had just told him.

My girlfriend Marcy arrived about half hour later and we all walked down to the car together. There was a big sign in the main lobby of the motel welcoming the Silver Eagles and I announced in a loud voice, "Hey, the Silver Eagles are here, doggone it, wish somebody had told me!" Johnny just shook his head in amusement. After he helped me get my stuff into the car, he kissed me goodbye.

"Don't forget, he said, "we'll be in Niagara Falls in a couple of weeks. Call me a week ahead and I'll let you know where we're staying."

Smiling, I said, "Can't wait," and kissed him. Nearby, the whole busload of Silver Eagles cheered. We hadn't realized they were all watching us. Marcy drove away slowly and I waved to Johnny as we pulled out of the parking lot. I then took a deep breath. Wow, things sure ended well this trip! Marcy looked over at me and told me that in the years she had known me, she had never seen me look so happy. We would see how the next trip unfolded. I knew down deep that everything could change in an instant.

15
Air Show: Niagara Falls

The next two weeks seem to drag by. Johnny and I had left Dallas on such a good note that I didn't think anything could possibly annoy me when I called him a week before the next show. I was wrong.

The first thing he asked me was how long I was planning on staying.

"Well, the trip's five days, isn't it?" I answered.

"Yeah, but are you going to stay the whole time? We don't want to spoil a good thing, do we?"

"Why don't we just play it by ear, okay," I answered, not wanting to start an argument. What the heck? Did he think he was going to get sick of me if I stayed too long? Honestly sometimes I felt like I was chasing a dream. Being with Johnny was either a high or a low. There was no middle ground. It was making me a little crazy.

This trip took some planning, as we had to fly into Syracuse and then drive three hours west to Buffalo. Donna wanted to go too, so I got her the cheapest ticket I could find. She complained the whole time about how much money it cost.

The motel they were staying in was just off the Interstate. We stopped at a coffee shop down the street so I could call Johnny. The team had just checked in and he asked me to come right on over. Donna was checking into the same motel and after she was settled, I excitedly took the elevator up to the third floor. Softly I knocked on his door. My heart was pounding. This trip was very important because I knew the end of the show schedule was near. If things didn't go well this time, time would pass and I might never see Johnny again. I said a silent prayer that this would be a great five days.

Johnny opened the door, grabbed me and kissed me all in one motion. He smothered me with kisses. I could hardly breathe.

"Do you remember that night at Dallas?" He looked at me seductively as we sat together on the bed. I couldn't help but smile as I thought back on that night.

"Of course I do," I said, "Why do you ask?"

"Are you kidding? Wow. That's the way love's supposed to be." He put his arms around me and pulled me down next to him.

"Honey," he continued in a whisper, "I want to make love to you, sure, but most of all I just want to hold you." I wrapped my arms around his back and marveled at how secure and safe I felt when I was with this man.

We made love slowly at first, delighting in the fact that we were together again. The days and weeks apart only made our time together more special and meaningful. Our lovemaking was getting better every time. I felt that we were connecting not just on a physical level, but on a spiritual one as well. It was mind blowing. Afterwards our hearts pounded together as we held each other tenderly.

"When you come like that, I know you're really mine," I whispered.

"Boy, you can say that again," he answered, kissing my face and blowing the beads of sweat off my forehead.

Soul mates. That's what we were. This kind of love only comes along once in a lifetime. We held each other for a few more minutes then reluctantly got up, took a fast shower together and went downstairs. Most of the fellows smiled as Johnny and I walked into the bar. Steve and Mike were standing at one end of the room with Donna right in the middle of them. She was trying to find out where Hank was, one of the guys she had been with at Clarksville. Steve said he'd go out and call him for her. Johnny and I shook our heads in amusement as we sat down at a table. He turned his chair so he was facing me.

"Hey Hon," I asked, "You're still so attentive to me and everything, how come? We just got out of bed."

"You goofball," he laughed, "I'm with someone I like to be with, that's all. If I just wanted sex, I wouldn't be here now." He leaned over closer to me. "When I'm with you, there's nobody else. I think you know that." I squeezed his hand and nodded. The whisper inside me stirred. I didn't like to be reminded there were other hole cards. I really tried not to think about that.

The jukebox was putting out some great tunes. Country music played a large part in our relationship and all the songs that played that night meant something to us. I had the most wonderful feeling that this night was going to be very special. We were dancing to the Carpenters song "Close to You," which we both loved, when I noticed Johnny looking down at me intently.

"Johnny, Honey," I said, "Why don't you just say what's on your mind. Can't you see what's happening to us?"

He dropped his arms. "I can't, Becky." He looked away from me. "I can't fall in love, not for a couple years, I just can't." I put my hands on his shoulders and turned him back around to face me.

"Would you like to have me disappear out of your life for a while and then suddenly just return someday?"

"I couldn't ask anybody to do that," he answered quietly as the music stopped and we went back to our table. He then turned me towards him and took hold of both my hands. "OK, I'll say it, but I can't make any promises. Understood?" I nodded silently. I suddenly found it hard to breathe. Johnny's words went straight to my heart. "I never realize how much I miss you until I see you." His eyes fixed on mine; neither of us moved a muscle.

"I love you, Becky. This is for real, you know, I've only said it once before in my life." I heard his words and emotion welled up inside me. I squeezed his hands and answered him quietly.

"I love you too, you know. From the moment I saw you at the first air show. I knew it instantly."

"Are you sure?" he asked, searching my face, as if he didn't quite believe me.

"Yes, I'm absolutely sure," I answered

breathlessly. "I've never been so sure of anything in my life."

Suddenly it was just the two of us lost in the romance of the moment. I was completely overcome with emotion and close to tears. Then Boom! Out of nowhere, Mike interrupted. "Hey you two! Knock it off! I can't believe how serious you guys are." Johnny shook his head and, with the mood broken, excused himself for a minute.

"Mike!" I exclaimed as he sat down next to me. I couldn't wait to tell him the news. "Johnny just told me that he loves me, how about that?"

"Been telling you that for months you dumb hammer," he answered. "It's about time you realized it for yourself." There couldn't have been anyone anywhere in the world any happier than I was at that moment.

We spent the rest of our first night at Niagara quietly talking about ourselves. Mike had the sense to realize that we didn't appreciate his company so he left us alone. I hadn't seen Donna since we first came downstairs so I guess she must've found Hank and gone off with him. There was no one else left to bother us. There was no one else to break the spell.

Mike did come over once to ask Johnny

when we were going to bed. "I'm staying in the room tonight, Johnny," he said, "so why don't you guys go upstairs so I can come up in a few minutes and get some shut eye?" I understood what Mike was saying as he didn't want to be in our room while we were making love. He didn't have another place to spend the night, and he was trying to give us some privacy.

"Do you mind if we just sit here and listen to the music?" Johnny asked sarcastically.

"Geez," Mike replied. "You're awfully romantic all of a sudden, Johnny, what the hell's got into you?"

Later, back at the room, we had our private time. Mike gave us an hour's head start and by the time he unlocked the door we were both out like a light.

Bus call for the boys this trip wasn't until two o'clock in the afternoon. This was great because it gave us all morning to be together. After we had lunch on the second day, Johnny and I dropped Steve and Mike back at the motel and headed for Niagara Falls.

Johnny had never been to Niagara Falls before. I had been there with my family when I was much younger, but I didn't remember much about it. It was like the first time for both of us. We walked arm in arm along the edge of the falls and I remember saying that the seventh wonder of the world might be Niagara Falls but the eighth wonder had to be the United States Silver Eagles.

As we leaned on the railing looking out at the mist, he whispered to me that to prove his love for me he would dive over the edge of the falls. He actually had stopped fighting his feelings for the moment and we were just like any other young couple in love.

"What the hell good would you do me down there?" I laughed, touched by his remark. Even though nagging doubt was still in the back of my mind, I pushed it away to enjoy this special time. One thing I knew for sure. I loved this man more than I ever imagined possible.

Amidst the sightseeing, music and private moments, the week was flying by. I could feel it leaving. This trip was much different from all the others. The air shows were in Canada so I didn't actually get to go to the show site. It must have had something to do with customs. No one explained and it didn't matter to me.

My afternoons were spent shopping, reading and just getting ready for Johnny's return. The beer was always on ice when he came back from work and I always welcomed him with a big hug and a kiss. I showed him in every way possible that he meant the world to me.

One night Mike met us in the hallway and asked where we were going.

"We're going to dinner, Mike, what's it to you?" Johnny replied.

"Dinner," smiled Mike. "You never take a hammer to dinner. Johnny, you must be in love." This time I winked at Mike.

The next night we all decided to go over to a bar to hear live country music. There was a three-piece band there with a pretty female singer. As I watched her, I made believe it was me up there on stage. Johnny noticed how I was completely into the music. He hugged me and said he was glad I was having such a good time. "You live in the right city, that's for sure," he commented. "Music City...Nashville."

By the time we got back to the motel, all I wanted to do was go up to our room and relax. We ran smack into Mike and Donna in the bar. I had forgotten that they had a date that night. I made Mike promise that he wouldn't bring her up to our room. Mike agreed and I hoped he was telling me the truth. Donna took me aside and told me she was leaving prematurely in the morning. She had a ride back to Syracuse and she had already changed her airline ticket. She said she was through with the Silver Eagles after tonight. I found that hard to believe but I wished her a safe trip and told her I'd see her back at home.

As Johnny and I opened the door to our room, he whispered, "I want to make slow love to you tonight, the way a woman should be loved. Remind me if I get carried away okay?" He was in a very romantic mood and I had come prepared. I changed into the sexiest nightgown I owned. Johnny's eyes almost popped out of his head when he saw me. I slid into the bed next to him knowing that this was going to be a memorable night. I had no idea at that moment how memorable.

"You know we have something very special, don't you?" I whispered to him.

"Sure Honey, don't you think I can tell," he murmured.

We had just started to make love when we heard a key turn in the door. I froze. "Johnny, damn that Mike! He's bringing Donna in here."

"Shhh, be quiet," he tried to calm me. "Lie down next to me and be still." Sure enough we heard Mike's laugh. Donna was asking if he was sure they should come in.

"I'll kill him," I whispered.

They stumbled into the darkened room and both hit the bed at the same time. Zippers creaked as clothes came off and I could swear I heard Mike breathing, he was so excited. Even though I was annoyed at Mike, this turn of events made things very interesting. Johnny decided, however, that I should not be exposed to this. He placed his hands over my ears so I couldn't hear anything but the faint squeaking of the bed. When it stopped, Johnny relaxed his hands. All was quiet in the next bed. We knew it was over.

"Now do you see the difference between physical love and the love that we have," I whispered. "That's two buddies in heat in the next bed. That's not what we have."

"You're absolutely right," Johnny whispered to me.

Apparently the excitement from the next bed had spilled over to ours. He made love to me quickly and urgently but for the first time since I had known him, I couldn't respond. I was too distracted. He rolled over and gently took me in his arms.

"I'll get Mike for this, I promise."

"Oh hell, Hon, forget it," I responded. "It's his room too. I guess sleeping next to us all week was just too much for him." We kissed each other goodnight and tried to sleep.

The next morning I woke up to the squeaking of the other bed. Johnny was awake too. He whispered, "Come on, let's get out of here." We quickly and quietly got up and threw our clothes on. We left the room immediately and I made it a point not to even glance over at Mike's bed.

Johnny had to go to work early because one of the aircraft had a mechanical problem. When we got to the airport, we saw the airplane sitting in the hanger with about five men in white coveralls working on it. They had grease from one end of their bodies to the other. Johnny told me they had been working on the airplane all night, trying to get it ready for the show.

"Look at them, Becky," he told me, "everyone thinks it's all glory to be a member of the Silver Eagles. They don't see this side of it." He explained that there were two spare airplanes in case of a malfunction or an accident. They both had the same safety checks and routine maintenance as the other six planes that usually performed at the shows.

I then sat in the car while Johnny finished what work he had to do. Every time one of the guys that I knew walked by, they would wave and smile at me. I felt like I belonged there.

When we got back to the motel we found that Donna had left, thank goodness, but Mike was still in bed. Johnny asked me to go into the bathroom so he could talk to Mike in private. I could hear everything anyway so it didn't really make a bit of difference where I was.

"How dare you bring that pig into this room," Johnny said very loudly. It was the first time I'd ever heard them argue.

"I never slept with anything that bad in my life. I'm ashamed of you, Mike." Johnny continued and wasn't through yet. "What the hell's the matter with you?"

Mike shot back. "Who the hell are you kidding? What about that fat tramp you had in Louisiana. Was she any different? It's just recently that you decided that every time you get laid it has to mean something. You never used to be that way."

"Well," Johnny bantered back to him, "at the very least you could have some respect for Becky."

The conversation ended abruptly so I opened the bathroom door and slowly walked out. Johnny threw a pillow across the room at me when I said something to tease Mike. Mike obviously wasn't too happy with Johnny. He was feeling hurt and he told me to mind my own business.

The next couple days passed by quickly. Too quickly. I remembered the conversation Johnny and I had on the phone the week before the trip when he wondered if I was going to stay the whole time. As it played out, there was never any question that I was staying for the whole trip. It was never even mentioned.

We made love every chance we got. It was as if we knew in our hearts that we weren't going to be together again. We wanted to savor the moments and burn them into our memories.

The next thing I knew, it was Sunday night and I had to leave first thing in the morning. We stayed in our room and just watched TV. The only serious question I asked Johnny was if he meant it when he said he loved me. I just couldn't put it to rest. I guess I didn't really trust it.

"Of course I meant it," he answered, "I can't say I like you, it's too weak." I smiled to myself as I appreciated his take on things.

"How come you said it to me now?" I asked.

He drew me to him. "I never felt like I

had to say it before."

"This is our last night," I whispered as I snuggled close to him.

He answered, "Sure, for this trip. Hey, what do you mean? Are you saying that you don't want to see me again?"

"Johnny, you're kidding right? You know how much you mean to me."

He hugged me but he was so tired he fell asleep almost immediately. As for me, I was awake all night because I knew this was our last night together. I was living in every precious moment. I watched him sleeping all night long.

Monday morning dawned bright and sunny. Quite the opposite of my frame of mind. Our time was drawing to a close. I took as much stuff down to the car as I could before the alarm went off. Johnny got dressed quickly and we walked down to the car holding hands. The silence hung over us.

This was the worst part of these trips, the saying goodbye. We both hated it. We sat in the car together for the last few minutes. Neither one of us said anything. I felt like I could cry at any moment. Finally I mentioned going to Vegas in a couple weeks. He avoided looking at me and said nothing so I just took that as a hint and kept quiet.

The rest of the Silver Eagles had already boarded the bus. It was time to go. He kissed me and looked deep into my eyes. "Take care of yourself and drive slow," he said as he got out of the car. I was so choked up, I couldn't even say goodbye. I just stared at him as he walked away from me.

"When Johnny, when?" I pleaded silently. This was the most painful of all the goodbyes. It felt different somehow because I knew it was.

That nagging doubt was still lurking at the back of my mind. As I drove out of the parking lot, I spotted him standing by the bus with Mike and Steve. They all waved at me. I watched Johnny in the rearview mirror as he stared at my car until I was out of sight. Was this the last time I would ever see him? Nonsense. I should feel calm, I told myself over and over. He loves me. I know it for sure now. He told me that he loves me. So why was I so certain that something was wrong?

The whispers were there and I couldn't push them away.

16
Rude Awakening: Phoenix

As I returned to my life and thought back on the five wonderful days at Niagara, the one thing that stood out from the whole trip was the fact that Johnny had told me he loved me. He told me for sure that I was someone very special in his life. The uneasiness I always felt was still there, however, and I didn't know how to make it stop.

Days went by with no word from him. The day came when my flight passes to Phoenix arrived in the mail. As usual I was ready to go at a moment's notice, but the notice never came. He never called and under the circumstances, the last thing I wanted to do was call him. If he wants me to go to Phoenix, he'll call, I reasoned.

Well, he might have called me, but now we'll never know because ultimately I didn't have the patience to wait to find out. I just could not help myself. I was driven to call him even though I knew it was the wrong thing to do. I dialed the familiar number in Phoenix. Once again I asked for Specialist Munroe.

Johnny came to the phone and was distant at best. I rationalized that he was always distant. He said that he didn't like the way his life was going. He was going to make some changes. When I had asked him what he meant, he said he didn't know yet. What on earth was he talking about? He promised to call me from the road the next week to tell me if he would be home during my vacation so that I could visit him. Even so, as I said goodbye and hung up the receiver, I knew something had definitely changed.

His ten-day road trip came and went. The Silver Eagles were due back in Phoenix on Sunday. I lasted twenty-four hours. I couldn't stand it. When I called him on Tuesday, at first he sounded happy to hear my voice. Then when I asked if he was going to be home at the end of the week, he shocked the hell out of me. I grabbed for a chair and sat down.

His voice was strong as he said, "Remember how I told you I had changed? Well, I sure have and you'll never believe it."

Something told me what was coming. I blurted out, "You're not getting married?!" Why on earth would I even think that, let alone say it?

"Yes, I am," he answered. "Remember the girl I told you about from Seattle? Well, I called her last night and she's flying out here Friday. We're heading to Georgia for the weekend to meet my folks."

The silence was deafening as I desperately searched for the proper words while trying to keep my composure.

"Johnny, you can't marry her after all that we've had together. Let me come to see you Thursday and at least talk to you. I won't try to change anything, I promise."

"No, Becky, don't come here, he replied. "It's because I care about you that I don't want you to come." What the heck did that mean, I asked myself. I pleaded with him to let me see him but I had learned a long time ago that when he said something, he meant it. There was no changing his mind. We both said goodbye and hung up.

Emily had made her way into the back room and was sitting at the desk opposite mine as I hung up the receiver. I just stared at her.

"That bastard," she said quietly. She had figured out the subject of the conversation even though she only heard my side of it.

"It doesn't make sense, Emily, he loves me. Why is he marrying her? It just doesn't make sense." I knew I sounded like a twelve year old. By this time all of the other girls had come back to see what was going on. I could see the sympathy in their eyes but the 'I told you so' looks were there as well. None of them had really believed that anything serious would ever come from our relationship.

Emily went out to the bar and got me a drink in a paper cup. I knew if I could cry, I would feel better. The tears would not come. I was in shock.

Slowly I began to think clearly again.

"Emily, I'm going to Phoenix whether he wants me to or not. I have to see him in person. Once he marries her, it'll be too late. He always told me he would only get married once. I have to try. I want to be the one. If I've already lost him, then there's nothing else I can do."

She shrugged her shoulders. "Okay, go if you have to. I can't stop you." She put her arm around me. "But remember your stock advice to everyone else when things go wrong. You always say that everything always happens for the best. Maybe for some reason this is the way it's supposed to be."

17
Swan Song: Phoenix

I had to see Johnny. I picked up the phone again and redialed the office in Phoenix. This time I asked for Mike. I ended up talking to both Steve and Mike. They both told me not to go. Yet something was driving me, pushing me, telling me to go out there no matter what anyone said. When Mike eventually realized how determined I was, he knew there was no stopping me and he agreed to meet me at the airport. I told him what time the flight was due and we hung up. No matter how things turned out, I thought I was doing the right thing by going there. I was a woman on a love mission.

The day of my flight dawned cloudy and gray like my mood. As I boarded the flight, I was on autopilot. It was like my actions were somehow being governed by someone else and I wasn't there at all. I was in a fog. Emily gave me some encouragement but I could tell that even she didn't think I should go.

I tried to prepare myself for all the possible scenarios. How would I react to Johnny when I was face to face with him?

Why couldn't I just be myself? Why did I think I had to constantly mold myself into something else?

Instead of sleeping on the plane like I usually did, I thought back over the last few months since I first met Johnny. My mind skimmed over some of the things he said to me when we were together. I would always remember these words, especially when he told me he loved me. Looking back on it, it was becoming apparent that this meant a lot more to me than it did to him.

My feelings and emotions were at an all-time high as the plane landed a half hour early. I looked out over the desert with its beautiful mountain backdrop and wondered if I was doing the right thing by coming here. The whispers inside me were strangely quiet. I dialed Mike's number and noticed how weird it felt not to dial the area code first. When Mike answered the phone, he said he'd be right over to pick me up. I found a spot near the front door of the airport and waited for him. Within a few hours this would be all over. I had checked the flight schedule and I could be on my way home tonight if that was the way things turned out. Or maybe he'd change his mind and ask to marry me instead. I prayed with all my heart that Johnny would want me to stay.

In what seemed like seconds, I saw Mike coming through the front door. I stood up as he came over to me.

"Mike, I'm so nervous," I said quietly as he hugged me. He wasn't the least bit optimistic either.

"Johnny might know you're coming," he warned me. "Joe asked me because he knew that I was leaving for the airport...and you know how tight he and Johnny are."

"Did you tell Joe that I was here?" I braced myself.

"No I didn't, but that doesn't mean that he believed me."

We got into Mike's car and headed for a nightclub close by. That's where they would be. Steve had been told to bring Johnny.

"Maybe when he sees you, it'll be different," Mike said, "but he asked yesterday if you were coming and told me that if you did, you were on your own."

We arrived at the club and got out of the car.

"Johnny's not here yet," said Mike glancing around, "so at least we have that edge." I felt like I was in a movie or something.

I asked Mike why he was being so nice to me.

"Hey, listen you dumb hammer," he said, "I like you and Johnny's my buddy. I think the two of you have something together. I'll do what I can to help you out, you know that."

I took his arm as we entered the club. The place was packed. A topless dancer stood on a small stage next to the jukebox and, interestingly enough, no one was paying any attention to her. There just happened to be two seats at the bar. After we sat down, he positioned himself to be able to see when someone else came in. No one was there yet. Mike told me to just sit there with my back to the door and he would let me know when they arrived. Suddenly he grabbed my arm. "Here they come. There's Steve, Slim and Joe...and Johnny."

He looked over at me. "For God's sake, calm down," he ordered. I tried to do as I was told. There was no sense to any of this. I was afraid I had made a big mistake coming here. I felt needy. Vulnerable. Out of control. What happened to the smart, cool, independent Becky? This was not my style. I wasn't happy about what being in love with this man had done to me.

They sat down at a table right behind us. Johnny was talking to somebody at the table beside him and hadn't yet seen us. Mike and I sat there for a few minutes of feigned conversation. Finally he said, "Come on, let's shake him up. Let's go over there." Like a robot I got up and followed him. This can't be happening, I thought to myself. I wouldn't make an ass out of myself on purpose.

Mike pulled out a chair for me between Joe and Steve. The surprised look on Joe's face showed that he did not know I was coming. Johnny was still talking to the guy at the next table and I couldn't tell if he knew I was there or not. Mike winked at me and went over and interrupted the conversation between Johnny and his friend. I saw the look of surprise come over Johnny's face and I wanted to disappear. There was nothing I could do but sit there and try to look comfortable. I wished I could hear the conversation between Mike and Johnny. Pretty soon Mike came back and Johnny resumed talking with the guy at the other table.

Mike stood next to me. "That Johnny is so damn stubborn. He must have the rag on, he's so miserable."

My heart dropped to my feet. "Why, what did he say?" I stammered.

"He said that I always wanted you and now I had you. I told him you came to see him but he won't listen."

He looked across our table to Steve. "He's mad because we didn't tell him she was coming," Steve explained.

"Oh the hell with him, Steve," Mike said, indignantly. "He might be my best buddy and all that but sometimes he's just too goddamn unreasonable." Then we all watched in stunned surprise as Johnny and Joe calmly got out of their chairs and headed for the door.

"Where is he going?" I gasped.

No one answered me as they walked right out the door. We could hear them drive away. I was in a fog. I realized that Mike was talking to me.

"Now I suppose you want to go over to his apartment and see him right? Don't do it, Becky. Don't give him that edge. We'll go out and have a ball, you and me. You don't need him."

I smiled at Mike. "Firing up to the last second, aren't you? You know I came here to see Johnny. I have to talk to him."

Mike gave in. He knew that my mind was made up. Shaking his head he said, "Girl, you're as stubborn as he is."

He silently got up and motioned for me to follow him. I said goodnight to Steve and we headed for the door.

Johnny's apartment was on the other side of town from the club. Mike and I hardly said a word as we headed there. What could I say? What could he say? There was no talking me out of it. I had to confront Johnny and get this settled once and for all. I would still have time to catch the plane back home tonight.

We arrived. My senses were on alert. The doorbells were lined up on the wall outside of a huge gate. An in ground pool was clearly visible, surrounded by doorways to the various apartments in the complex. I pushed the button to apartment #5 and waited as the gate automatically opened. Mike came with me as I pushed open the door to the apartment and walked right in. Johnny was standing there in the hallway. I marched right up to him fully intending to call him every name in the book for ignoring me at the club. Instead I stood there dumbfounded as he extended his hand, smiled and said, "Becky, baby. I didn't know you were here. Would you like a drink?"

What? I thought, what is going on now? I glanced over my shoulder and noticed that Mike had gone back outside, shutting the door behind him.

I turned back to Johnny. "Johnny, you could've at least talked to me."

147

"Oh yeah, well, why didn't you tell me you were coming? How come you called Mike?" His voice was raised.

"What? Because you told me not to come." I too was trying very hard not to yell at him.

He handed me my drink. "So what. You still should have called me. I can't believe you came here after I told you not to. But it's good that you did."

I had no idea what he was trying to say. I sat down on the couch and looked around the apartment. There were Silver Eagle pictures all over the place. It was a typical guy's apartment with just basic furniture, a bar on one wall and a color TV and stereo system on the other.

"I know you can't believe I'm getting married," he was saying, " but I realized after the last road trip that I really love this girl. She's finally getting her divorce. Imagine this, I didn't have sex with a single hammer on the last trip. That's when I realized I loved her. I called her as soon as we got back Monday night."

At that point Joe nonchalantly entered the apartment to get a drink. Johnny then disappeared into the bedroom.

"Joe, what is going on?" I asked. "Is he

for real?"

Joe shrugged his shoulders. "All I know is that she called him Monday night. Whether they'll get back together or not I can't tell you."

" Well," I said, "that's a different story than what he just told me. He told me he was marrying her."

"Well I guess he knows what he's talking about," Joe answered, avoiding my stare and then going back out the door as fast as he could. I realized Johnny was lying to me. After that big speech the first night we met when he said, 'No lies.' Johnny came back into the room and sat down next to me. He tried to explain.

"I know you want me to say that you never meant anything to me," he said. "Then you can tell all your girlfriends what a son of a bitch I am. Okay, I'll say it. You never meant anything to me...but you know I don't mean that. I told you when I was with you that there was no one else. But that was when we were together. You weren't supposed to go home from a trip with me and dream about the next one. No, that wasn't what I meant when I told you I loved you."

"But Johnny," I replied, "it's different for us girls. We just can't turn it off and on like you do."

"So be it," he answered, "but I'm marrying her and that's that."

"Johnny, if you love me," I said quietly, "How can you marry her?"

"You told me if you came here you wouldn't try to change things," he said as he got up and stomped into the kitchen where he quickly mixed another drink. He came back to me. His tone had changed. "Can't we just be friends?" he said softly.

Friends? I was so confused I started to cry. "Johnny, I just know you won't marry her, you'll see."

"Oh yeah, what...did the stars tell you that?" he sneered. "Hey, before I forget, DJ's marrying that Capricorn hole card he told you about." Double whammy. Really Johnny, I thought to myself, you have to tell me that now?

I looked at him in disbelief. I had finally had enough. A strange sort of peace came over me. My eyes stung from crying. My head had started to ache from all the screwdrivers. I was completely and utterly exhausted. Suddenly all I wanted to do was get on a plane and go home. I looked over at Johnny who was now sitting on the other side of the room watching TV. It was pretty obvious that he thought this whole subject was closed. There would be no further discussion.

Just then Mike opened the door and called in to me, "Come on Becky, your plane's leaving soon. We've got to leave right now."

As I walked by Johnny's chair, he reached over to the table next to him and picked up the book I had given him in Dallas.

"Here," he said gently, "I guess you don't want me to have this now." I grabbed it from him and put it in my bag. That little book that had meant so much. He didn't want it anymore. He didn't want me anymore.

I turned back to him as I reached the door. He had followed behind me. His eyes searched my face. "You always said Capricorn and Aries weren't compatible," he said quietly. I couldn't respond because there was nothing left to say. I simply picked up my stuff and opened the door. Mike went out ahead of me and slowed to wait. I forced myself to look at Johnny in an effort to say goodbye. His face looked worn and tired.

"Goodbye Johnny." I was trying to be kind and not break down. It was difficult to speak. He touched my arm and said quietly, "Goodbye Beck." I shut the door behind me and realized that this was the only time since I had known him that he didn't kiss me goodbye.

Mike cautiously took my arm and asked if I was okay. I just shook my head and walked with him silently to the car. Mike, as usual, was looking out for me. It was clear that he was downright pissed at his best friend. He could hardly contain himself.

"Wait until I come back here after I drop you off. I've got a few choice words for that lame son of a bitch. I swear to you, Becky, he's going to be sorry one day and I hope you get to laugh in his face. I would never let a hammer like you go. Never in a million years." Mike always did have the ability to make me laugh. I smiled weakly at him through a cloud of tears and thanked him for all the times he had my back. He said, "I've still got your back, you know. Don't give up on him. He'll come around but it might take longer than you're willing to wait."

We rode the rest of the way to the airport in silence. My mind was blank. I was having trouble processing everything that had just happened. As painful as it was, at least there was some closure and I had the chance to say goodbye.

When Mike pulled up in front of the airport's main door, I turned and kissed him on the cheek. "Thanks again for everything Mike. If you're ever in Nashville, I'm in the phone book. You know I wish you happiness and love. I've always wished this for you." He put his arm around my shoulder,

"You're one hell of a hammer, Becky. It was fun having you around. You take care."

I got out of his car and never looked back. Inside the Phoenix airport, I checked in for my flight and boarded my plane. I barely nodded to the crew and was relieved that I didn't recognize any of them. I collapsed into my window seat, relieved that there was no one sitting next to me. As the tortured lyrics of love and loss from Karen Carpenter's "Superstar" filled the cabin, I leaned my head against the window, closed my eyes, and fell into a fitful sleep.

In the blink of an eye, we were landing in Nashville, and my time as a Silver Eagle hole card had come to an end.

18
Six Months Later: Nashville

Emily Davis was my best friend in the whole world. She came to pick me up that awful night when I came home from Phoenix. We had decided to share an apartment to save money and I was so happy we were roommates. It helped me now, when I really needed the support that she had to offer me. After all, she knew the whole story from beginning to...end. We spent a couple days rehashing everything that happened until I just didn't want to talk about it any more. She helped me to see that my world had not stopped turning because of Johnny Munroe.

Things like this are lodged so deep in the heart that it can take awhile for the head to process. While I tried to rid myself of the memories, I couldn't stop my thoughts from going over and over and over it again. I had lived in the moment with Johnny and was amazed how I was able to remember every last detail. Each and every memory replayed in my mind. I started writing them down. The first day in Miami. The boarding pass flying off and

154

landing at Johnny's feet. The joy. The frustration. The need. The pain. The surrender. I wrote and wrote and wrote. Chains of memories. My life with him was like a maze. I kept writing down my memories in an effort to try to figure out where it all went wrong. I had enough fodder for a book. One day, several months later, I found I had successfully purged every memory by writing it down and letting it go. It was the key to my healing, but it had also become a full manuscript, a diary written after the fact, of our love affair from beginning to end. I was ready to leave Johnny Munroe behind in the archives of my life. I took all the pages, all the pictures, the boarding pass, and every memento from my love affair with him and packed them neatly into a box. I hid the box even from myself, not ever wanting to open up the wound and memories again, and put it high up on a shelf in the spare closet. I even put the little book, the one I had made for him, at the bottom of the box. I felt relieved and was prepared to continue on with my life.

Emily and I started going out after work. It was time to have some fun again! We lived in Nashville, after all, where the clubs were filled with live country music every night of the week. I had always dreamt of being a country singer so it was easy to imagine that it was me up there on the stages of the clubs, singing my heart out. Life was good and I did my best to move on and not think about Johnny or the Silver Eagles.

Music can be a powerful and interesting thing. It made me forget everything else. But it made me remember too, for every once in awhile I would hear a song that would bring me back to the times we shared and I would pause and remember him. It was like he was buried deep inside my heart. Over time Johnny became a distant memory as my life became my own again. Surrounding myself with Nashville's music and new way of life was a good way to move on and forget Johnny Munroe.

A few months later a friend called out to me from our break room at work, "Hey Becky! Did you see the newspaper today?"

"No, Chuck, I didn't. What's going on?"

Chuck started reading aloud a story about the Silver Eagles. "...The Silver Eagles had an accident during one of their shows...the pilot had to eject from his aircraft. While the pilot made it safely to the ground, the plane was demolished. No one on the ground was hurt..." For just a moment I could clearly remember watching the air shows and holding my breath. "Hey," he added as he approached me at the ticket counter, "have you ever heard from that guy you were so crazy about?" I shook my head in response. "Why don't you just call him?"

"I don't know if he's married," I replied. "I don't want to call him."

Chuck looked thoughtful for a moment. "Do you have the number for the Silver Eagle compound in Phoenix?"

"Yes, I have the number," I answered. "Why? What are you going to do?"

Chuck replied, "Let's find out if he's married!"

Emily had walked by and heard the last sentence. She came over to us, saw the look on my face and burst out laughing. "Let him call," she said. "They won't know it's you and then maybe you can put this Eagle thing to rest for good. I know you've still got some feelings for him even though you've tried your best to move on."

Reluctantly I gave him the phone number.

Chuck was a great kidder and practical joker. I found myself hoping that Johnny was away on a trip so Chuck wouldn't be able to talk to him. He dialed the number and put the phone on speaker so we could hear too. When the secretary answered, he asked for Specialist Munroe. She told him that Johnny was out on a trip for two weeks. I started to breathe easier. Thank goodness he wasn't there. She asked if she could take a message. Chuck made up some story that he and Johnny had worked together before Johnny joined the Silver Eagles. He asked how Johnny was doing and then nonchalantly wondered if he was still married. Emily grabbed my arm. I think she thought I was going to keel over or something.

The secretary answered, "Oh yes, he's very happy."

Chuck made a face at me as he said thanks, nice talking to you, and hung up the phone. My first reaction was to laugh when I pictured the scenario of Johnny trying to figure out who Chuck was. But then it hit me. Johnny had gotten married after all. Everything he said that last night in Phoenix was true.

I turned to Emily, who was surprisingly quiet. "It's finally over, he's married," I said. She put her arm around me and said, "This was his loss, not yours."

19

Music City USA: Nashville

Emily and I had a favorite place to hang out after work called The Hummingbird Cafe. Along with live music, they featured an Open Mic night once a week where local people could go up on stage and sing with the band. I had heard there were a few local artists who made it big after being discovered here. After all, this was Music City USA! You never knew who would wander in at any given moment from the record business.

The marque said, "Open Mic Night" as we arrived one evening. Emily was always bugging me to go up on stage and sing. The only place I had ever sung anything was in my bedroom at home with the stereo up so loud that no one could hear me. A lot of my childhood was spent making believe I was a country singer. I would lip sync the songs on the radio and make believe I was on a stage.

When I was very young, my mother insisted that I take piano lessons even though I was only four years old. She wanted me to be a concert pianist but I didn't like that kind of music. I was finally able to quit my lessons when I was eleven because I rebelled by chipping the paint off the front of the piano. I can still hear my mother crying as she told my father about it. He told her to leave me alone and he would take over my musical training. That's when he bought me my first guitar. I was so excited when he taught me how to play. When I picked up that guitar, I became a different person. My shyness went away and I became strong and confident.

As we walked into the bar at The Hummingbird, we could see that everyone was in a great mood and enjoying the music. The band started to play one of my favorite songs and Emily and a couple others dared me to go up on stage. Before I knew what was happening, they practically carried me up there and plopped me in front of the microphone. I remember looking out at all the people, feeling sick with stage fright.

I heard Emily yell from the audience, "You can do this Becky!"

Someone handed me a guitar and then everything changed. I stepped up to that microphone like I had done it a thousand times. It seemed as natural as breathing. The bass guitarist nodded to me and I started to sing. Thankfully, I knew the song and the words. After stumbling on the first line, I relaxed a little and started to enjoy being on the stage. It was a popular song and the crowd started to sing and clap along with me. When it was over, everyone yelled and applauded and I smiled and waved.

Emily met me as I walked off the stage. "Wow, Becky, you can sing. Who knew?" I was beaming from ear to ear.

"I've always wanted to sing on stage and I can't believe I had the nerve to do it. Thanks for making me."

Emily hugged me. We had a drink and enjoyed watching the others perform. Emily whispered to me, "You're the best one." I smiled and told her she was crazy.

It was late when we got ready to leave. As we walked out the door to our car, I made myself a promise I would do this again. Soon.

About a week later, we stopped in on the way home from work. We had just sat down at a table when a handsome older gentleman came over and asked if he could join us for a minute. Sure, we said, not knowing who he was. It turned out he was the owner of the club and he remembered me from Open Mic night. He wanted to be sure I'd come back the next night and go up on stage again. Apparently people had been asking him if he knew who I was. I was flabbergasted and didn't know what to say but I assured him that I would be back the following night. He asked our names, shook our hands, and went back to the bar. He told the waitress to bring us a drink. His name was Marty.

Emily was practically jumping out of her chair. I reminded her that we had come there to relax. "This doesn't mean anything," I told her. "He's just being nice." She rolled her eyes and told me not to kick a gift horse in the mouth.

All of a sudden I had a million questions. What should I wear? Where are my cowboy boots? Should my hair be worn down or up? WHAT WOULD I SING? Emily told me to calm down. We would figure all of this out. At work the next day I could hardly concentrate on what I was doing. I kept imagining myself singing on that stage.

As usual, the bar was crowded the next night when we arrived. We had both noticed that most of the people that sang on Open Mic night were men. Maybe that's the only reason Marty asked me back, I thought, I'm something different, plus I'm wearing a short skirt. I figured that couldn't hurt.

Marty was waiting at the door for us. He put his arm around my shoulders and guided us to a table right near the front of the stage. "Have fun, Becky," he said. "You'll be up in a few minutes. I see you brought your own guitar this time." People, mostly men, were crowding around the stage in front of us.

We sat down but I was too nervous to order anything. Emily asked me what I was going to sing. I had no idea. The band was playing mostly current songs and I knew most of them. When Marty introduced me a few minutes later, I had calmed down and was prepared. Everyone clapped as I took a deep breath and walked out onto the stage.

The bass player who had seemed to take me under his wing asked me what I wanted to sing. I chose a Rascal Flatts hit, "Bless The Broken Road." He called the song out to the drummer and the other guitar player. They gave him a thumbs-up and he nodded at me, on cue.

Again, as long as I had my guitar, I wasn't afraid. It was actually fun! When it was over, the crowd yelled for more and we agreed to do an encore song. People were actually standing up and clapping for us! This was blowing my mind.

My time was up and I walked back to Emily and sat down at our table. People were walking by telling me how much they enjoyed my music. Emily was bursting at the seams. Marty came over to our table and asked me if I would meet with him the next day. He approached me about being a regular on Friday and Saturday nights. They had been looking for a female singer for a long time. I couldn't find my voice for a minute I was so surprised. Joy surged through me. It never dawned on me to ask if I was going to be paid.

Every little girl in Nashville dreams about this! I couldn't help but imagine the possibilities! I knew it was a long way from here to a record deal but I was thrilled I was going to get the chance. I listened for the whispers inside of me. They were silent. I took that as a good sign and told him I'd see him in the morning.

20
Twenty Years Later: Nashville

It was a rare and treasured night off. I was at my computer, lost in thought with one ear on the TV as I was waiting for American Idol to start. I found myself thinking deeply about the years that had passed and how much had changed since that first Open Mic night at The Hummingbird Cafe. No way. Twenty years? The time seemed to have flown by and yet so much was different now. I was different.

Life at work had changed too. Despite several tempting opportunities along the way to take early retirement, Emily and I were both still working for the airlines. I remembered how easy it used to be to schedule trips with the Silver Eagles that summer, but over the years it had become increasingly difficult to schedule my work days around rehearsals and singing commitments. I was still juggling my job while singing at The Hummingbird on the weekends. My singing was my priority and I still had dreams of stardom. Sometimes I would be asked to fill a spot in another club and I always jumped at the chance. After all, the more people that saw me, the better.

I was so naive when this all began. Way back then I thought I'd sing a few songs and be discovered, just like that. I never dreamed that twenty years later I would still be waiting. Hundreds of country singers in Nashville were still paying their dues and I was one of them. I was very lucky to have a steady gig and I knew it. It never mattered to me that I wasn't being paid. Marty was my manager and had become a good friend. He always insisted that I was something special. We were constantly looking for the right song to break the ice and to pave my way to the charts.

I thought how country music had changed over the years. The genre had progressed from being called country western to just plain country, embracing versions of country rock and country soul. Kenny Chesney and Tim McGraw were becoming household names. I had stayed on top of the changes and found that I loved this new country, which featured lots of new artists and many more female singers. It took some effort to keep up with everything, but I adapted my style with the changing times and I hoped that one day that it would pay off.

One thing never changed. Emily, my friend for life. I could always count on her. We still lived in the same apartment complex and, even though we weren't roommates any more, we continued to spend a lot of time together. She always supported my singing commitment and helped me in any way she could. She always was, and always will be, my very best friend. Emily had married an airline pilot along the way, but they divorced some years later when she caught him having an affair with a flight attendant.

Another thing? Despite all the changes and time that has passed, no one I ever met could hold a candle to Johnny Munroe. Once a year on his birthday, I allowed myself a brief moment to remember him and wish him well. I could see our time together through different eyes now and genuinely hoped he was having a happy life.

It was interesting to look back and see how much I had changed. I had mellowed over the years and was grateful for the experiences that had brought me this far. Would I ever marry again? The dream of finding another love was still alive inside my heart. As the years passed, my thinking had shifted on soul mates. When I was with Johnny I thought there was only one soul mate in each lifetime. I always believed that everything could change in an instant, for I had personally experienced that, and I had come to believe that it is possible to have more than one true love in your life. Suddenly my mind drifted back to the Silver Eagles and Johnny. I hadn't realized yet that something on television was triggering a memory that would come to change my life further. The power of music was preparing to impact me once again.

21
SUPERSTAR: Nashville

I was jolted back to reality. One of the American Idol contestants had chosen a melody from the 1970's. I sat, spellbound, listening as Karen Carpenter's ballad, "Superstar," filled my living room. It had been so very long since last I had heard it. I reached for the phone to call Emily but she was already on the phone calling me. "Hey, Beck, are you hearing what I'm hearing?"

I softly answered her, "Yes, I hear it." I was lost in the haunting music and the lyrics from so long ago. This was the music that reminded me of Johnny and our precious times together. I honestly had not thought of him except on his birthday in many years. It seemed strange to me that for some reason I had been thinking about him just moments before.

The next week American Idol was on again and this time I was talking on the phone with Emily just as one of the favorites was getting ready to perform. We both let out a little cry when another female singer started to sing the very same song by The Carpenters. There were the haunting words from "Superstar." Again.

"Becky, Becky, do you believe this?!" Emily was as shocked as I was. I couldn't help but wonder if this was some kind of sign. My mind grappled with the enormity of this. The contestants never sang the same song twice in one season, yet here they were! As I pondered this, two light bulbs went off in my head at the exact moment.

Quickly I hung up on Emily and called Marty, interrupting him on his night off. This was really important! I told him that I must talk to him first thing in the morning for I knew I had found the song we had been searching for. It was right under our noses! I hung up the phone with him and called Emily back.

"Emily, come over here!" I yelled into the phone as I dropped it in my haste. Music stirs our memories like nothing else. It now reminded me of the volumes I had written so long ago. How could I have forgotten? Where was it? The manuscript! The book! The box! Did I even still have it?

I raced upstairs and climbed high up on a chair to reach the top shelf in my spare closet. There it was. High on a dusty shelf, the yellowed manuscript had been waiting for the right moment to be revealed. Finding it with a smile, I dusted it off and hurried eagerly with the pages back down to the living room. Even my favorite TV show faded away from my awareness as I became absorbed and soon found myself reliving my own incredible love story. I opened it carefully and smiled when I saw the pages I had thoughtfully typed, double-spaced, so long ago. In the very bottom of the box I found the little book that I had made. The one I gave Johnny before he gave it back to me. Seeing it brought a tear to my eye.

Emily meanwhile was racing over to my apartment. She called out to me as she ran through the front door. "Are you all right?" She was very concerned. "What on earth is going on?"

I couldn't talk. I just waved the pages at her. I couldn't wait to reveal the manuscript to her. She sat down next to me and grabbed some of the pages out of my hand. Her eyes were as big as saucers as she realized what she was reading.

"You wrote this? You actually wrote everything down? All of it? Becky, I don't believe it. Why didn't you tell me!!"

For the next few hours we both laughed and cried as we read the story. We opened a bottle of wine and became totally engrossed in reliving that time so long ago when we were so young and carefree. I could not help but be appalled at some of my actions and the choices I had made. One thing was abundantly clear. My life as a hole card revolved around Johnny. I was vulnerable and innocent and would have done anything to spend time with him. When we broke up, I was too immature to understand that when someone wants to be out of your life, you just have to let him go.

There were many times my intuition had kicked in to warn me or alert me but I ignored the whispers because I was so enthralled with this man. Over the years I finally learned to listen to my feelings and the insightful whispers that came from deep inside of me.

I wondered if things might have turned out differently if I had had more self-respect and had been more honest about some of my feelings. Maybe I should have taken leave of him now and again instead of always being the one left behind. In hindsight, I could see how much I had changed and grown over the years. It was hard to believe that the young woman I was reading about in the story was actually me. At the same time, it was the strangest thing...as I was reading the manuscript, I could feel the power of the emotions from so long ago as if it were yesterday.

Reading my story, the love between Johnny and me felt as real as it ever did and the pain of losing him hurt just as much. As I read the final chapters, I believed once again with all my heart that Johnny had really loved me. It all came rushing back to me. It made me wonder about him. Had he been able to find another love like ours? I knew I hadn't.

Emily and I hugged each other as we read the end of the story. We both had tears in our eyes. I piled all the pages back in the box on top of the little book. I wasn't able to bring myself to look at that little book.

"Wow, first you're singing and now this! I didn't know you were a writer! A writer and a singer. How about that!" She laughed, "Who knew you had so much talent?"

"I'm as surprised as you are," I told her.

Then I excitedly shifted gears and told her what I was thinking about. The song. "Superstar."

"This is it Emily! We've been trying to find a breakout song for years and it's been right there all along. Now I'll just ask Marty to help me get into a recording studio. People all over this town must owe him favors. I know I can do this! The emotion is still there and it's the emotion that will sell the song." Emily looked at me wide-eyed and agreed that yes, this could be the break that we had been waiting for.

She left for home promising that she would return first thing in the morning. I washed my face and went to bed exhausted and overwhelmed with emotion. What had just happened? I felt my life changing again. After trying to relax for what seemed like hours, I finally slept soundly until morning.

22
The Big Break: Nashville

As promised, Emily arrived the next morning before dawn. I could hardly open my eyes but somehow I managed to take a quick shower and get dressed. Enthusiasm bubbled up inside of me as I thought about telling Marty my idea. Emily wanted to talk about the manuscript. She was bursting with questions.

"So how do you feel after sleeping on this?" She hardly took a breath as she asked me questions faster than I could answer them. "Do you still have feelings for Johnny after all this time?" She paused as I poured us a cup of coffee.

"Emily, I can't answer that right now. This whole thing makes me uncomfortable. I'm still trying to process the powerful feelings that have been aroused from reading the manuscript. Give me a few days at least."

Emily agreed. We then stopped talking about the past and began to focus on the future. The first thing I had to do was talk to Marty. I finished my coffee and told Emily I'd see her later.

As I walked into The Hummingbird, I noticed how different everything looked in the morning light. The cafe was almost deserted except for a few people sitting around drinking coffee. Marty was waiting there for me and told me he wasn't convinced that a song from thirty years ago would catch on in this day and age.

After talking about this for a while, we agreed to give it a shot. I would perform "Superstar" that Friday night and we would see how the crowd responded. There would be plenty of time to rehearse with the band later today.

"I'll give you a chance, Becky, I owe you that much."

I thanked him and quickly called into work to take an emergency personal day. There was nothing more important than this! No one asked what was going on and I was glad I didn't have to explain what I was doing. My airline job, which had supported me all these years, was now taking second fiddle to my music. There was a lot of time to go home and think about what had just happened. I realized I actually had a shot at making a name for myself! I firmly believed this one song was the key to everything.

As it sunk in, my nerves were getting

the best of me. Emily tried to reassure me. She could see how anxious I was. Later she drove us back to The Hummingbird and she made sure I didn't forget my guitar! The three-piece band that I had performed with over the years was waiting for me when we arrived. They were all talented musicians and I was very lucky to have them to support me. When we were on stage together, they made me feel more confident. Kenny, Carson and Luke all told me I'd do just fine. They would make sure of it. Marty came in from the back office to watch the rehearsal. There was a feeling of excitement in the air.

The band tuned up and we were ready to go. The rehearsal went off without a hitch. We got it right the first time but did it again to be sure. Marty was impressed. I asked for a backup singer to harmonize and Marty readily agreed. He was pleased, I could tell. When we were finished, he came to each one of us and shook our hands.

"Good work all of you," he said. "Let's see how it goes Friday night. I'll get that backup singer for you, Becky."

I thanked the band and hugged them all. We had become good friends over the years of working together. Marty then walked us out and said he had a good feeling about all of this.

Emily told me that we definitely had something. Of course I already knew that and could hardly contain my excitement. We went home and had some champagne to celebrate. Big things were coming. I could feel it.

23

Undercover: Perry

The next morning I decided to put the music on hold for a couple days. My curiosity had been aroused as my memories came back to life through my manuscript. The search was on. I was determined to find contact information for Johnny and Mike. Emily arrived to help and we found an address for Johnny in Perry, Georgia, just south of Atlanta. There was no way to find out if it was current. There was no information to be found on Mike anywhere. We also found some old pictures of the two of them when they were Silver Eagles. They looked so young!

"Do you think we'd recognize them now?" Emily asked. I couldn't help but smile. In those days I thought anyone over thirty-five was old.

"Just because we're in our forties and still gorgeous doesn't mean they have aged well too. It doesn't matter, though, because we'll never see them again."

"Unless...unless we make a trip to Georgia!" Emily was practically jumping up and down with excitement about her idea.

"Are you saying, Emily, that we should go find Johnny?" I was not amused.

"Just to see what he looks like!" Emily responded, "Not to talk to him or anything." I couldn't believe I would even consider the idea.

"How would we find him? This is stupid," I replied.

Emily responded, "It's such a small town, everyone probably knows everyone else. We'll find him."

She whined a little more, so I humored her and told her that I'd at least think about it.

She had always been this way. Once Emily got something in her head, there was no stopping her. Once again, she was on a mission. She bribed Chuck at work all week with coffee. She begged him to call the number for Johnny that we had found online. Our first goal was to make sure he was still alive, and then to find out if he actually lived there. After all these years, Chuck was still our go-to guy when we needed information. I wanted no part of it. "Just let me know what you find out," was all I could say.

It always amazed me how people will just talk to strangers on the phone. Chuck managed to find out that Johnny and his son lived at that address. Don't ask me how he got this information. I haven't a clue.

Then Emily was relentless. I finally agreed to fly to Atlanta with her, rent a car, and drive down to southern Georgia. I found a black wig from my younger days and stashed it in my bag. Emily borrowed one of my blonde wigs. I had to admit there was a twinge of intrigue and excitement in the air. The next day we boarded a flight to Atlanta where we rented a car and drove south for about an hour. This was only going to be a one-day trip no matter what. The flight back to Nashville was at 7 pm. I was glad I wasn't singing at The Hummingbird until Friday night.

It was around noon when we arrived in Perry. I couldn't help but smile every time I looked over at Emily in the passenger seat with her blonde wig and sunglasses. Then when I looked in the rearview mirror, I didn't recognize the person with black hair looking back at me. It sure was a good disguise!

We referred to a computer printout, which showed us where Johnny lived.

"I guess we can just drive by his house," I said to Emily, adding, "Do you realize how crazy this is?"

Emily smiled. "You never know, Becky."

Perry had one stoplight, a gas station, a hardware store, a post office and a diner named, "Mama's."

"Where does everyone buy groceries around here?" I wondered aloud.

It was not difficult to find Johnny's road, as it was the first turn off from the main road. I felt like we stuck out like a sore thumb with a rental car. About two miles up the road was a sign that said that we were approaching Black Stone Lake. There weren't many houses but I noticed a bunch of rural mailboxes with house numbers and names on them. There it was. My heart began to pound. There on a silver mailbox: MUNROE 365. Suddenly I felt very anxious. Across the road from the row of mailboxes were some lovely condos on the shore of the lake. Emily, who had been unusually quiet, perked up.

"He must live in one of those beautiful condos!" she said. "Must be nice." We didn't need to be ace detectives to figure that out. There didn't seem to be any people around the homes. If they were outside, they must have been down by the lake. I drove to the end of the dead end road and turned around.

"Now what Emily? This was your idea, remember? I'm not going to go knocking on doors." Emily didn't respond.

We pulled off the road and parked down by the boat launch. What a nice place to live, I thought to myself. These condos aren't cheap. We sat there by the lake for about an hour, watching people come and go. It was definitely an exclusive community. No one in particular caught our eye. I was beginning to think this was a total waste of our time.

"Let's drive back to Atlanta. We've got some time to hit a few stores before we catch our flight," Emily said quietly. Was she was giving up after bringing us all this way?

We headed back toward the main road and decided to stop and have some lunch. The wigs stayed on. There were a few cars in the parking lot at Mama's and country music could be heard blaring from inside the diner. We walked in and sat in a small booth with a red tablecloth. Music was coming from a portable stereo. There was a short counter with a few empty bar stools nearby. The lady that took our order wore a green tee shirt that said "Mama's." I wondered if she was the owner. We ordered turkey sandwiches and coffee.

I looked across the booth at Emily. "You insisted we do this, you know. Well, if nothing else, it's still a nice day for a drive through the beautiful Georgia countryside."

Emily agreed but quietly added, "Just wait, it's not over yet." What on earth did she think was going to happen?

We finished lunch and got ready to drive back to Atlanta. We left a tip on the table and stood up to pay the bill. Out of the corner of my eye, I saw the screen door open and two men in jeans walk in. They sat at the counter and said hello to the lady in the green tee shirt. Emily saw them at the same time I did and sat right back down.

The lady asked, "What will it be today, John, as if I didn't know?" It was obvious she knew him well.

The man smiled and said, "Hi Sarah, my son and I will have our favorite, Georgia peach pie and ice cream." My breath caught in my throat as I recognized that smile and heard that voice and those words. Time virtually seemed to stand still.

Georgia peaches. The memory flashed back to that night so long ago when Johnny told me how special this pie was to him.

I found that I had to sit down too. My legs were like jelly. I put my sunglasses on as a big surge of emotion welled up in my chest. Was I going to scream or cry? I didn't know. I stole a glance at Emily who had already put on her sunglasses. She was trying very hard to hold it together. She couldn't look at me. Meanwhile I was staring at Johnny and his son and felt my eyes filling with tears. Johnny Munroe was sitting ten feet away from me and yet there was nothing I could do. I couldn't bring myself to talk to him. How would I ever explain being there?

He was even more attractive now that he had a few years on him. Damn, men always seem to age better than women. His son was the spitting image of what his father looked like twenty years ago. This whole thing didn't seem real. It felt like a crazy dream.

I motioned to Emily to stand up so we could quietly leave as soon as their orders came. I prayed I wouldn't stumble as we walked by the counter and left the money for our bill by the cash register. They were totally oblivious to us as we went out the door. Neither one of us I made a sound as we walked to the car and got in. As we drove out of the parking lot, Emily asked me if I was all right.

"How can you even ask me that?" I answered. "I just saw the biggest love of my life, and I couldn't even speak to him. I don't know how I feel right now but I probably shouldn't have let you talk me into coming here."

A few minutes after we drove down the road, I had to pull over. We had to talk about this. What were the odds of him walking in like that!? Emily was surprised and pleased that her plan had worked. I choked back the tears and couldn't help but think about how wonderful it might have been if things had played out differently. We finally took our wigs off. Emily drove us back to Atlanta and we caught our flight to Nashville. I just wanted to go home. It had been a roller coaster of a day.

It was late by the time we arrived home. Emily had to work the next day but I didn't, thank goodness. The drama of our trip to Georgia had done me in. I took a hot shower and went right to bed. Sometime during the night I had a dream about Johnny. It was one of those dreams where you know what is going on because you're consciously in the dream. He was standing in the parking lot at Mama's when I walked out the door. Even though he looked strange, I knew it was him. He called out to me to stay. I started walking away from him as fast as I could. I could hear him talking as he followed me. He called out to me again. He told me that the biggest mistake he ever made in his life was letting me go. So how about that? Had Mike been right after all? In the dream, I reminded myself this was only a dream. I turned around and told him it was too late. Too much time had passed. He reached out and tried to grab my hand. I pulled away and woke myself up. My heart was pounding and I could feel the passion in my body from just being near him. It didn't matter that I knew it wasn't real. I lay there quietly until I got my bearings and then got up to get a drink of water. It took quite a while for my body to calm down. I wondered...what the heck is going on? I figured that it was just a reaction to seeing him that day. I was shocked that he would reach out to me like that. It was so real it was hard to believe it was only a dream. Were the whispers inside me trying to tell me something?

"Where have you been for the last twenty years, Johnny Munroe," I screamed silently.

Eventually I calmed down and went back to bed. I wondered what Emily would have to say about this. After a while I went back to sleep and was relieved that there were no more dreams.

After I filled Emily in on the dream the next morning, she was unconcerned and told me to just forget about it. She didn't think it was a big deal. My emotions had become a jumbled mess and I knew it would take time to sort it all out. That dream had my attention. I reluctantly realized that I had unresolved issues that had bubbled to the surface. It was hard to believe that I had carried all this around for so many years. Emily understood when I explained what I was feeling. She said that I hadn't even mentioned Johnny for many years so the stuff that was buried must have been very deep down inside of me. I was glad that I could finally face these feelings and let them go once and for all.

I found my priorities competing with each other, so I tried to set it all aside to focus on getting ready for my big night at The Hummingbird. The question of the day: Would the audience like "Superstar?" My music career hinged on the answer. Rehearsals went smoothly. Marty even had a backup singer in place. We were ready to roll.

24

Opening Night: Nashville

It was Friday night. Emily had to work so I didn't have her support for my big night. She promised she would stop in for a drink on the way home. People were waiting in line as I arrived. My name was even on the marquee! I was so nervous! I snuck in the side door and quickly walked to the back of the stage. I wanted to talk to the band before we played our first set. They all told me to calm down and just have fun. Marty hugged me and wished me luck. "You'll do great, Becky!"

The band warmed up with a fifteen minute set without me. I used that time to make sure my makeup wasn't smeared. Looking in the mirror, I smiled at my image. My white cowboy hat looked classy and I was glad I'd had my blonde hair highlighted.

It was time. The big crowd was clapping! I took a deep breath and told myself I could do this. As I walked out on stage, I waved at everyone. The butterflies in my stomach started to calm down as Kenny, the bass player, handed me my guitar. We had decided to start with another Carpenter song, "We've Only Just Begun." The crowd responded favorably so we paused for a few minutes and then continued on with "Superstar." My emotions took over as I sang the beautiful lyrics of love and heartbreak. Johnny was very much a part of me for those three minutes. My eyes were filled with tears as the song ended. As I bowed, the audience erupted in cheers and applause. They were going crazy, chanting they wanted another song. I quickly went backstage to pull myself together.

We had rehearsed one more Carpenter song, "Close to You," and it ultimately went off without a hitch. My backup singer was right on key on all the songs. She was amazing. We then took a break for a few minutes before going back for a second set. Marty was high fiving all of us. The band picked the songs for the rest of the night and I went along with whatever they wanted to play.

Marty was beaming from ear to ear when we finished. He agreed with me that "Superstar" was the song we had been looking for. Emily arrived in time to see our last set. She hugged me. "I knew you could do it."

Marty said we would talk the next night. He was going to make a few phone calls. Emily and I had a nightcap and then we left. I could hardly talk I was so excited. We realized that things were looking good. Maybe a recording contract was in the works.

The next day Marty called me and asked if I would come over around lunchtime. Of course I agreed and I couldn't wait to hear what he had to say. When I got there he told me he had called in a few favors around town and had gotten a recording company to let me record a three-track debut CD of the Carpenter songs. The name of the album would be "Rebecca Steele Sings the Carpenters." The deal was such that I wouldn't be paid anything until we saw how the public responded. He would try to market the first cut, "Superstar" to country radio, which was the key to everything. He said he would take care of all the paperwork involved. I would be signed to a short-term contract if all went well.

Marty then introduced me to the record producer who had come to meet me. He shook my hand and welcomed me to his company. Mr. Parker wore a big black cowboy hat and expensive cowboy boots. He looked the part. The name of the record label was "Dream Big Nashville." I thanked Marty for going to bat for me. We all agreed to cut the debut album the following week. Marty reminded me to make an appointment with a photographer for professional pictures for the album. This was happening! Almost too fast.

I literally floated out of the meeting. I had made up my mind. After going home and sharing the news with Emily, I went over to the airport and signed the paperwork to accept an early retirement package. Thank goodness the offer from the airlines was still available. It would give me the freedom I needed to pursue my music career. Everyone was very supportive and wished me the best. The girls said they wanted to organize a small retirement party for me. It sounded wonderful and I thanked them. It never dawned on me that I was taking a huge chance, leaving the stability of my job and all. I was absolutely positive that it was the right thing to do.

Marty had arranged for a sound technician to record "Superstar" there at the club before we recorded it in the studio. He wanted to get it to country radio as soon as possible. He told me that it wouldn't be as crisp as the actual studio recording but it would sound just fine.

He was right. Within a week, country radio in Nashville had picked up "Superstar." Billboard even mentioned it in their up and coming news section. It was just a matter of time until it would be released nationally. I kept pinching myself to see if all of this was real. "Superstar" would come to be the most asked for song in our sets at The Hummingbird. Apparently a lot of people could relate to the raw sentimental lyrics of this song.

Meanwhile, I was improving and learning about the music industry by leaps and bounds. So far everyone had been supportive and helpful. I hoped it would continue. I was looking at it with eyes wide open for I had already learned that it was tough to be a woman in this business. I had to bite my tongue on occasion and ignore the sexist remarks that often came my way. To keep some semblance of privacy, I changed my phone numbers and made sure they were unlisted. Mr. Parker was told not to give my phone number to anyone without checking with me first.

A few days later, I noticed him standing at The Hummingbird bar when I arrived. He walked over to me to say hello and told me about the success of my single "Superstar." It was such good news! He wanted Marty and me to go to his office the next day to talk about a record deal like he promised. He wasn't even going to wait until the debut album was recorded! Oh, and by the way, he had a message for me. Seems someone had called him asking for my phone number. He stuck to our agreement and wouldn't give my number out to anyone. He said the person left a message and that it was 'very important'. He handed me a piece of paper and I thanked him for taking the message.

Marty came over to us and I shared our good news. We all shook hands and agreed to meet the next day. It only took twenty years to get this far. Imagine that.

We were due on stage in a few minutes so I put the piece of paper backstage with my stuff and totally forgot about it until later that night.

25
Passions and Priorities: Nashville

By the time I left The Hummingbird to go home that night, I was exhausted. There were a lot of visitors from out of town in the crowd and we tried our best to make them feel welcomed. My throat was a little sore so I was glad I wouldn't be singing for a few days. I dropped my stuff on the table by the door when I got home and wondered if Emily was home from work yet. I was just about to call her when I spotted the piece of paper Mr. Parker had given me. It had fallen onto the floor at my feet.

I wonder what this is, I thought as I picked it up. It read, "Call Johnny Munroe: 555-545-2343."

My mind flashed back to over twenty years before when I received the same message. Johnny had called to ask me to meet him in Dallas. It was the only time he had ever called me. I stared at the piece of paper and found my way to a chair and sat down. It took me a minute to figure out what was going on.

He must have heard my record on the radio and because my numbers are unlisted, he called the record company to try to reach me. You think you're pretty smart, Johnny Munroe, I thought, but I don't want to talk to you. I crumpled up the piece of paper and threw it in the trash. I called Emily but she wasn't home yet. Shaking my head, I took a hot shower and went to bed. The phone rang about twenty minutes later. Emily was calling, wanting to know how the night went. I told her about the record deal and she wanted to come over to celebrate with me.

"We can celebrate tomorrow after the papers are signed," I told her. Then I mentioned the message from Johnny. She was shocked and insisted I call him back. I told her we'd talk about that tomorrow. I was too tired to even think about Johnny Munroe. This had been quite a day.

Sometime in the night, I realized that I was much more excited about the record contract than I was about Johnny calling me. There was a time when I would have given anything to hear from him. Time had changed things, a lot.

26
The Dream Comes True: Nashville

Marty called me the next morning inviting me to join him and Mr. Parker for lunch. I didn't have to work at the airport until late afternoon so I agreed to meet them at noon. Phew, two more days and my airline career would be over! No more time conflicts. It would be a welcome relief.

We met at a very nice restaurant away from music row. Was Mr. Parker trying to impress me? When Marty picked me up, I asked him. He said he thought Mr. Parker just wanted to treat us to a nice lunch; no strings attached. I laughed and said, "Oh Marty, there's always strings attached."

Marty smiled knowingly. "You sure seem to understand the way things really work in this crazy town."

When we were seated and had ordered our lunch, Mr. Parker told us he would like to sign me to a two year contract for now. I would only be required to cut one album per year. I was confident. With the wealth of talented songwriters in Nashville, I knew I would be able to find good songs. He would have some say in the venues where I performed, but he also wouldn't stop me from using my own judgment. Marty negotiated the money part of the contract. I trusted him to take care of me. He was now not only my manager and friend, but he was my agent too. After all these years, I would finally be paid for performing my music.

Mr. Parker asked if I had any requests before we signed the contract. The only thing I wanted was to be sure that the band at The Hummingbird was on board too. They had been with me the whole time and I wasn't about to leave them now. Mr. Parker agreed and said he would talk to them later that day. I knew they would be thrilled. We then signed the contract and shook hands. Our food order arrived and we had a nice lunch with the business part out of the way. It felt almost like we were all old friends. It felt right.

On the way home, Marty asked me how I was doing with everything that was happening. I told him it was impossible to put my feelings into words. My dream had finally come true and I was very grateful. I thanked him for believing in me all these years.

Not once did I think about calling Johnny. That ship had sailed a long time ago.

27
Raising the Bar: Nashville

Emily was acting kind of weird the following night. She was insisting that we go out after work to celebrate the signing of my contract. I didn't want to do anything but go home. It was my last night of working for the airlines. The years had gone by in a flash.

Finally I agreed to go out with her but insisted that we make it a short night. When we drove over to The Hummingbird, I was shocked to see the marque with the words, "Congratulations Becky!" There was also a message that announced a private party. After ten o'clock the club would be closed. I didn't have a clue. I asked Emily what was going on.

"Silly you. Marty closed the club to give you a proper celebration. What a cause for a party, you're leaving the airlines and entering show business! Woo hoo!" No wonder she had been so insistent that I go out after work.

We walked in the side door and saw the balloons and decorations everywhere. It was colorful and festive and I was very touched that the girls from work had put this all together for me. Even people from the record label were there to meet me and shake my hand. Marty had hired a band from another club to provide the music and drinks were on the house. I couldn't help but think how much money this was costing and I realized it foreshadowed the world I was stepping into...the world that was quickly becoming my life.

There was a big cake on the table by the bar that had a picture of a singer drawn in frosting on the top of it. Chocolate, my favorite. Everything was perfect. Things looked like they were finally going my way. The music was loud and upbeat. Everyone was dancing and enjoying themselves and before we knew it, it was closing time. I made sure to thank every single person for being there and gave Marty a big hug. I had tears in my eyes as I said goodbye to all the people I had worked with at the airlines for so many years. There were a lot of great memories.

Marty told me we would be recording the debut album in two days. Two days! I told him again how much I appreciated the great party. He said goodnight to us and said he'd see me at the recording studio. Emily and I walked out slowly and I realized my life was about to change dramatically. On the way home, we talked about flying over to Hilton Head for an extended vacation after the album was cut. She said she'd ask for a leave of absence the next morning. Life was good and we both knew it.

As Emily dropped me off, she asked me if I was going to call Johnny. "No," I told her. "I couldn't even if I wanted to because I threw his number away." She shook her head and said, "I hope you're not sorry one day you did that." I could've cared less. Nothing was more important to me than the record contract.

The next day I had my hair straightened and my picture taken for the album cover. I insisted on wearing my white cowboy hat for one of the pictures. Emily helped with my makeup. Later I smiled at the image of myself in the mirror.

My recording session was scheduled for ten o'clock the following morning. We all met at The Hummingbird and rode over to music row together. Marty spent a few minutes with us explaining all the legal stuff before we went inside. There were more papers and releases that had to be signed before we recorded anything further. This business was very complicated.

I noticed the statue of Elvis Presley and his guitar in front of the studio across the street. That was the studio where he had recorded his music. I had taken a tour of it when a friend was visiting and remembered being in that building. There was even a picture of me sitting at Elvis's piano. Who knew I'd be recording my own album on the same street one day!

This recording thing was a totally new experience for me. I had never even worn headphones before. The sound technician in the next room kept trying to make me laugh so that I would relax. Everything went well, considering. My backup singer had a lot of experience and told me to just pretend I was on stage.

We recorded all three Carpenter songs and were finished in a couple of hours. Then we went out to lunch to celebrate and to wish each other good luck. I knew I wasn't dreaming but it sure felt like it! How about that ...I had just recorded my first CD.

After lunch we all said goodbye and I told Marty I was going to be leaving for Hilton Head Island. I assured him I would return to Nashville and that I would honor my commitment to him and The Hummingbird. When I got back, I would begin choosing the songs for my first major album.

Emily and I high fived each other as we arrived home. Everything was just humming along.

28
Synchronicity: Hilton Head

A few days later we were on a flight to the island again for some rest and relaxation. By the time we landed, got our rental car and arrived at the condo, most of the morning was gone. It was a beautiful warm summer day and we decided to take the bikes out and go for a ride on the beautiful trails that passed through the whole island. A short distance down the beach from the condo was a brand new club with a huge outdoor bar and a big restaurant. We agreed we could probably roll home from there.

Our first couple of days were divided between the beach club and the bike trails. There was no shortage of things to do and places to go. The beauty of the island was breathtaking and there were so many restaurants to choose from.

"We better stop eating out so much," I told Emily, "it's too easy to gain weight here!"

She laughed and said; "We're putting lots of miles on the bikes. We'll be fine."

We decided to go over to the other side of the island for dinner a couple nights later.

The restaurant and bar had live music and great food. It was already crowded by the time we got there. There were a few people waiting to be seated, so we had a drink at the bar while we waited for a table. For some reason Emily began to reminisce about our crazy side trip to Georgia a while back. She was still laughing about wearing those wigs! I was not as eager to talk about it and was glad when we finally got seated for dinner. We ordered another drink while we looked at the menu. Nearby, the maître de was calling out names for open tables and booths.

We had just been served our salmon dinners when the music stopped and we heard as plain as day, "Munroe. Party of two. Your table is ready." We looked at each other and shook our heads in disbelief, almost afraid to check out who walked up to the counter. We were in the back of the dining room, so we had a view of the whole place. We both watched to see who answered the page, expecting a man and a woman. From the bar area, two men walked up to get seated. Had they been in the bar when we were there?

"You have got to be kidding..." I said to Emily, whose mouth was hanging open. I don't know which one of us was more shocked. There was an uneasy feeling in the pit of my stomach. We recognized the men as Mike and Johnny as they walked up to the counter together and were then seated across the room from us. We tried to enjoy our dinner, but by then we had both lost our appetites. We ordered another drink and tried to decide what, if anything, we should do.

"I know, I know," said Emily, who always had a plan. "Let's buy them a drink when we leave, and leave our names on a paper napkin."

"No way," I told Emily. "I don't want Johnny to get the idea I want to see him. After all, I never called him back. We can send them a beer, if you want, but no names. Let them try to figure out who we are." Emily agreed that this was a much better idea.

"Okay," I said, "let's tell the waiter to send the drinks over when we leave. By the time they get them, we'll be long gone."

I could hardly wait to leave so we could play our little trick. I gave the waiter $20 to deliver the two beers. "Can we call you in about half an hour to see what they say?" I asked him.

"Sure," the waiter answered, "I'm Larry. I'll be glad to fill you in."

We quickly left the restaurant so we wouldn't be seen.

"We're like two kids, aren't we?" Emily laughed.

We drove back home which gave them enough time to finish their meals and leave the place before we called to see how it all went down. Larry answered the phone on the first ring. He laughed as he told me how they had both jumped up and ran to the door. "I told them two hot babes bought the beers. They seemed like they were eager to find you. "
I thanked him for his time and hung up.

"Emily, this means they are on this island somewhere. Are we going to be looking over our shoulders now the whole time we're here?"

"Not me, Becky, "she answered, "this is a big place. We'll probably never run into them again."

I had left my cell phone on the counter at the condo and didn't realize there were two messages from Marty and one from Mr. Parker until it was too late to call them back. Whatever was up would have to wait until morning.

29
More Opportunities: Hilton Head

The next morning I called Marty bright and early.

"Are you sitting down?" he asked me.

"What's up?" I couldn't imagine what he had to tell me. As he spoke, his words didn't register with me at first because I thought he was joking. He assured me he wasn't.

"People are hearing 'Superstar' on the radio and you're becoming a household name." He continued. "An interesting call came into Mr. Parker's office from ELLEN's personal assistant. Ellen DeGeneres just so happens to be doing a show about people starting entertainment careers late in life...and she wants you on it! How about that!"

The goose bumps started and didn't stop for five minutes. Marty said that Ellen would send a crew to The Hummingbird if I didn't want to go to California to appear live on her show.

"Becky are you there...say something please."

"Tell me you're not kidding," I replied. "This would be a very mean practical joke, Marty."

He assured me again that he was telling the truth. "You have time to think about it, Becky. They don't need an answer right away. The show is three months out."

I thanked Marty for telling me and left a message for Mr. Parker. Then I yelled for Emily to come downstairs. People all the way to the beach club could hear her screaming when I told her. We talked about it for a while and I realized what a huge break this could be. Of course I would do it. ELLEN, can you imagine?

A couple nights later, we decided to go over to the beach club for a nightcap. Where did all these people come from? A lot of people on vacation, I thought, for it was very crowded. There was a beautiful circular bar in the middle of a huge room with direct views of the ocean. First class all the way. In contrast to a lot of the bars in the area, this one was quiet. Soft music was playing in the background. I was thinking how it would have been a great place for a romantic evening. Emily and I sat at the bar and raised our glasses in a toast. "To our friendship and all the adventures ahead of us." We clinked our glasses and settled down to enjoy our brandy.

A group of men were talking across the bar from us. We noticed they were in a very animated conversation and were laughing a lot. We both saw them at the same time. I grabbed Emily's arm. Mike and Johnny didn't see us. They were deep in conversation with the other men.

"Do you want to leave?" Emily asked, poking my arm.

I thought about it for a minute and replied, "No, let's just see what happens."

We hadn't seen each other for twenty years. Would they even recognize us? I eventually couldn't stand it and told Emily to go over and say hi to them. Out of the two of us, she was the one with the nerve. I wanted to hide under the bar.

She said, "Here goes nothin,'" and bravely marched right on over to them. I watched it all from across the bar. I heard her say, "Excuse me, don't I know you from someplace?"

Their laughter cut through the room like a knife as Johnny and Mike realized who she was. She pointed over to me and it seemed that Mike couldn't get to my side of the bar fast enough. He hugged me and said, "Damn it, Becky, you're still one beautiful hammer!" I was really glad to see him.

Johnny and Emily took their time walking over to us. I didn't know what to do. I mean the last time I saw him we broke up and I was a mess. Should I lie and tell him I never got his phone message? Is the "no lies" promise still in effect after twenty years? I didn't think so because I remembered how he didn't keep his part of the bargain.

When they finally came over to us, you would have thought we had seen each other yesterday by the way Johnny casually said, "Hey, Becky, good to see you, how've you been?" He never mentioned that he called. He didn't touch me. I was glad because I didn't know how I would react.

Emily sat down next to me and Mike kind of stood between us. Johnny excused himself to take a phone call and was standing a few feet away. To say this was awkward was an understatement. I looked at Emily and said bluntly, "Let's get out of here." Just then, Johnny walked over to us, said goodnight and told us he had to leave. It was the strangest thing. You would have thought we were strangers. Mike, on the other hand, was just bubbling over with all kinds of questions and information.

We soon finished our drinks and stood

up to leave. Mike asked for my cell number so we could keep in touch. He was renting a house about a mile away and Johnny was visiting so he'd be around for a while. I put my hand on his arm and told him I was glad to see him. I told him that he still looked like a movie star. We all laughed like we used to and it didn't seem possible twenty years had gone by. I asked what was up with Johnny and he said, "I'll fill you in the next time I see you." Mike seemed sincere. He said goodbye to Emily who was standing by the bar waiting for me. He kissed me on the cheek and winked at me as he turned and walked away. Johnny was long gone.

Emily and I walked home along the beach. There were too many thoughts running through my head to even talk. I had always believed there were no coincidences. Why we were all brought together again was beyond me.

30
Catching Up: Hilton Head

The next morning Emily left early to catch a quick flight back to Nashville. She had an appointment there and would be flying back later in the afternoon. I was just taking my coffee outside when my phone rang.

"Good morning sunshine!" It was Mike, up bright and early too, wanting to come over to 'catch up'. Johnny had gone back to Georgia the previous night after his phone call. Apparently there was some kind of family emergency.

"Come on over," I told him. "Emily's not here. She'll be back later. I can't wait to hear everything that's been going on all these years."

It took him just a few minutes to arrive. He walked around the condo and came up on the deck from the ocean side. We sat outside and enjoyed the view of the ocean while we drank our coffee. Mike said that he had heard that I was a big singing star now.

"Not quite," I laughed. He told me that he remembered how much I liked country music.

"So," I started, "What's the story with Johnny?"

He smiled and said, "We don't have all day so I'll make it brief." He went on, "I know you remember that awful night in Phoenix when I dropped you off at the airport..."

I nodded (how could I forget) and he continued.

"Well, I went back to Johnny's apartment like I said I would that night and let him have it, both barrels. He didn't speak to me for a week."

"Are you going to tell me what you said?" I asked quietly.

"Sure, I'll tell you. I told him he just made the biggest mistake of his life and that he would live to regret it. I told him he'd never find another hammer that loved him as much as you did."

I looked over at him and smiled. "You always were my biggest fan, you know. So tell me, were you right?"

"Damn right I was," he answered. "He got married to that girl he told you about and stayed with her for about ten years before he threw in the towel and left. He told me he hated to admit it but it looked like I was right about you after all."

I sat there, dumbfounded. "Then why

didn't he try to find me?"

"He did," Mike replied. "He talked to somebody where you worked and they told him you had gotten married. It killed him but he didn't want to interfere."

This was news to me. Nobody had ever told me that Johnny had called. I told Mike that I had been engaged but had called off the wedding. Why would anyone tell him I was married? For a moment I imagined how different my life might have been had I gotten that phone call. What if...

Mike waved at me. "Hey, are you with me, Becky?" I'd been drifting.

"Yes, it's just a lot to take in. What happened next?"

"He stayed single for a couple years and then he tried again. This one didn't work out either, so he just gave up and has stayed by himself pretty much ever since. There's usually a hammer around if he's lonely."

I shook my head. "I'm sorry things didn't work out for him."

Mike snapped, "No, you're not. You told him he'd be sorry and it turned out he was. I told him too but he was too pig-headed to listen."

I asked if Johnny had any children. Yes, he had a boy from his first marriage. A boy. I remembered his son at the diner in Perry. I sat there trying to process everything in my head while Mike went inside to get us more coffee. This was a lot to digest. It didn't change anything, though. I didn't trust Johnny and I did not want to have anything more to do with him.

Mike came back outside and asked me how I felt about all that he had told me.

"Things have a way of working out the way they're supposed to," I said. "If I was meant to get that phone call that day, I would have."

Then I wanted to know about Mike's life. Did he get back with his wife?

"Yes, as soon as my tour with the Eagles was over, we got back together. I stopped drinking too. We have two sons. We were together until she passed away a couple of years ago." Tears stung his eyes as he told me this. I got up, walked over to him and hugged him.

"I'm so sorry, Mike. I'm glad you had a wonderful life together." He thanked me, returned my hug and stood up.

"Enough of this serious stuff, Becky. Let's go for a walk on the beach." It sounded like a great idea, so off we went.

The time flew by as we laughed and

joked the whole way. By the time we turned around and reached the beach club on the way back, we were both starving. We stopped to have lunch and then headed back to the condo. Emily would be back any time.

It was easy to be with Mike. He laughed a lot and it was good to see he hadn't lost his sense of humor. It was fun to talk about the times we had spent at the air shows. We made it a point not to talk about Johnny.

When we got back to the condo, Emily was just coming in the door from her trip. She saw us and gave me a strange quizzical look like she wondered what was going on. Mike greeted her and said he had some things to do and that he had to leave. I thanked him for the great day and told him to come back soon. He winked at me like he always did and walked out the door.

Emily asked me what we talked about and I filled her in on Johnny's life. She said, "I knew it. He screwed up, that's all. Oh well, his loss." She was shocked that anyone we worked with would have kept secret the fact that he had called me.

"I suppose we'll never know who it was. Doesn't matter anyway. Water under the bridge."

She was sorry to hear about Mike's wife

and wondered why he hadn't remarried. "Most guys can't stay alone for five minutes, let alone five years." I had to shake my head at the way she phrased things.

My phone was on the table and I noticed I had a voicemail message waiting for me. I dialed in and Marty's voice came over loud and strong. He said he had two important things to tell me. He had booked me into a club in Atlanta two days from now. They had some sort of a new artist night and he thought I should be part of it. The second thing was that I had been invited to sing at the Ryman Auditorium in Nashville this weekend. What an honor this was and I was thrilled! Emily hugged me and said that she'd go with me. I called Marty back and thanked him for both opportunities and told him I'd fly to Atlanta the day after tomorrow. He gave me all the information and wished me luck. I remembered to tell him to book me for the Ellen show. I would be happy to fly to Los Angeles and appear in person.

"Come on Emily, I've got to go find something to wear! Off we went to go shopping. I ended up finding a cute outfit with a fringed short skirt and a sequined vest. I even bought red cowboy boots. I called them "my lucky boots" and decided to wear them whenever I was on stage.

Mike called first thing the next morning. He couldn't wait to see us to talk about the old days and the Silver Eagles. He said Johnny had called wanting to know if he had talked with us. He told him he had spent the day with me and yes, we did talk about him. Mike told him it was no use because I didn't want to see him and that I had no feelings left for him. He said he didn't think Johnny was going to give up. Mike then came over and spent the afternoon sitting with us at the outside bar of the beach club. We were drinking margaritas and I hadn't laughed like that in years. Mike had excellent recollection and still had his twisted sense of humor.

"Do you remember how I would come into the room in the morning and you had a sheet pulled up to your neck?" Mike was laughing so hard he could hardly talk about it. Emily had never heard this and she laughed so hard she cried. It was funny for me too, of course, but a part of me remembered how embarrassing it was.

"What about the time I brought that friend of yours into the room while you were in bed with Johnny?" Even after all this time, I remembered that night vividly.

Emily said "WHAT?" and then we all

convulsed in laughter again. This went on for hours. It was a perfect afternoon.

I told Mike about my big plans for the week. He was very happy for me and said this could turn out to be a big break. Before he left, he teased us by saying that he had a plan and would fill us in when I came back from Nashville.

"What are you talking about Mike?" We were hanging on the edge of our seats.

"Hang tight, I'll tell you soon." He winked at us and off he went.

31
Paving the Way:
Atlanta to Nashville

Emily helped me to get ready for Atlanta. I was so grateful that she could go with me. It made me less anxious to have her there. We were able to catch a flight in the early afternoon the next day. Marty had booked the hotel room and arranged for transportation from the airport. The club I was appearing in the next night was a block away from the hotel and we could walk there easily. I learned that each new artist could pick one song to sing. There were about fifteen of us scheduled to perform.

Emily and I checked into our hotel and scheduled spa treatments for the next day. We had an early dinner at the hotel restaurant and called it a night. The next morning we had a scrumptious breakfast and then enjoyed our spa day. We both felt like we were on vacation. The nerves started to kick in as I was getting dressed for my performance. We got there early and met some of the other artists. I realized I was one of the lucky ones because I already had a recording contract. We all met with the band to make sure they knew the arrangement of the songs we wanted to sing. There was no doubt I would be singing "Superstar." My turn came fast. Before I knew it, my name was called to go up on stage. There were a lot of people in the audience. I was glad I knew the song so well. Someone handed me a guitar and the butterflies disappeared just like always. This was my first gig away from The Hummingbird and it was life changing. I was wishing I could stay on that stage for the whole night. The tears were there at the end of the song and I knew I had connected with the audience.

There was a lot of applause as I waved to the crowd when the song was finished. People were standing next to the stage wanting autographs! This surprised me, as this had never happened at The Hummingbird. Emily called me a celebrity as I walked off the stage. I was in seventh heaven. We walked over to the bar, smiling and shaking hands along the way. I told Emily people thought she was an artist too. I knew she got a kick out of all the attention.

We found two seats at the bar and ordered drinks. A strange feeling came over me as we sat there talking to people who were walking by. Emily was chatting with one of the other performers when I realized someone was staring at me. I turned in my chair and my heart jumped in my chest. Johnny was standing right there next to me and nonchalantly asked if he knew me from somewhere. Before I could answer him, Emily spun around and said, "What are you doing here, Johnny Munroe?" I asked him the very same question. Even though I knew he lived close by, it never entered my mind that he would show up here. Mike must've told him about the show.

Here he was, still so handsome it took my breath away. He complimented my singing and said he remembered the song well. He wondered why I had never told him I played the guitar. I could feel myself getting sucked back in by the same old feelings. He asked me if I wanted to go someplace quiet so we could talk. I managed to say no and stood up to go to the ladies room. Emily was right behind me.

"What are you going to do?" she asked. I answered that I was not going anywhere with him but that I needed to talk to him before we left. I hoped to be strong enough to walk away from him.

We returned to the bar and saw that Johnny had found a vacant booth for us. Emily sat at the bar and didn't take her eyes off us. As soon as I sat down, Johnny ordered another drink. He remembered I drank screwdrivers. He told me how great it was to see me and wanted to know if I would leave with him and stay at his home for a few days so we could get reacquainted. He told me he didn't live far away, that he lived on a beautiful lake. Oh, I know where you live, Johnny, I thought to myself as I had a flashback of sitting at Mama's. Wouldn't you just die if you knew we were there that day at that diner sitting ten feet away from you?

I told him I would be singing at The Ryman in two days and that I was going back to Nashville in the morning.

"Come on Becky, don't you remember how great we were together? It can be like that again." He got up and moved to sit down next to me in the booth. When he put his arm around me, I cringed and shrunk into the wall to get away from him. He got the message and took his arm off me. From somewhere deep inside, these words came pouring out of me. It didn't sound like my voice.

"I remember everything, Johnny. I remember it was always about you, everything was always about you. Guess what! I'm not blowing my big chance to sing at The Ryman to go anywhere with you. This time it's all about me."

He looked shocked and didn't speak. I glanced at Emily who was grinning from ear to ear, motioning that we should leave. I stood up and Johnny moved out of the way. He didn't try to stop me. Emily and I walked out of the club without even saying goodbye. Emily high fived me when we got outside. I was shaking in my red cowboy boots. I was wishing Mike had been there to witness it. He would've loved it. I think he would have been proud of me. Emily wanted to talk about what had just happened and said she was impressed with how I stood up to Johnny. I felt light and carefree as if a tremendous weight had been lifted off my shoulders. We walked back to our hotel and put a Do Not Disturb sign on the door. Sleep came easily. We flew back to Nashville the next morning.

Singing at The Ryman a few days later was a dream come true too. As I reveled in the tradition of this beautiful historic place, I could feel the presence of those who had gone before. "Superstar" echoed off the walls and brought me to tears.

My friends were there to celebrate with me. Mike came along to be sure Johnny didn't show up to spoil my big night. He was not surprised Johnny had come up from Perry to see me sing in Atlanta. "I thought he might do that," he said. "It's so close to where he lives." He laughed his head off when Emily told him how I told Johnny off. He said he would have loved to have seen it. "Good on ya, Becky, now when he asks you to marry him, you can laugh at him." I remembered Mike had said those very same words to me many years ago.

32
A New Kind of Show:
Hilton Head

Everything returned to normal fairly quickly after we returned from Atlanta. I was toying with the idea of telling Mike about the trip Emily and I had taken to Perry but decided it would be better if I kept my mouth shut. I remembered how Mike always liked to be the one with the scoop. I knew he would run and tell Johnny.

We were having coffee one morning a few days later when he started to tell me his idea.

"Mike, are you crazy? What do you mean we're going to pull a con on Johnny?" I was staring at him in disbelief. "What are you planning? Or do I even want to know..."

Mike smiled at me. "Hang on Becky, I've got it all figured out. Remember long ago that night in Atlanta, the night he thought we slept together? He went nuts over that. Remember he called you? I know you must remember, because I do." He continued, "His feelings for you have never changed, even after all these years and everything that's happened. I understand, though, why you don't believe a word he says. I don't blame you."

"What are you up to Mike, you crazy son of a bitch."

Emily came in from the deck, intrigued by what she was hearing through the screen door. "Let him talk, Becky, he knows Johnny better than anyone."

"Okay, here goes," said Mike. "Emily, you have to be in on it too. And one other person, and I'll tell you in a minute who that is." I sat down and found myself completely mesmerized by what Mike had concocted.

"We're going to play a charade, the three of us, for two months. We're going to tell Johnny that you and me, Becky, we're getting married." I almost fainted and Emily couldn't stop laughing after she spilled her tea all down the front of her.

"Just listen," Mike continued. "It's payback time! There's no way he'll let you marry me and then you'll believe him once and for all that he honestly and truly does love you." He paused to take a breath and to see if we were still with him.

I eventually found my voice. "How the devil are we going to pull this off?"

He answered, "It'll be awesome. We'll

figure it all out as we go along. He'll stop the wedding, you can bet on that, if he doesn't do something beforehand. He knows you don't trust him now so he'll have to come up with something big to convince you." Mike was grinning from ear to ear. "This is going to be a blast, you'll see. But you two can't give it away. You've got to be cool about it or you'll ruin the surprise. Are you in?"

I had to admit, as crazy as it sounded, it might work. Johnny had told Mike he had been trying to figure out a way to get me to give him another chance, but he knew I just couldn't let my guard down with him. It was no surprise that Emily was just as excited as ever. She was practically jumping up and down.

"See! I told you! I knew you and Johnny would get back together somehow!"

I was trying to make sense of this plot. "The only way I can do this is if Johnny never sees us together because I'd never be able to keep a straight face. How are we going to do it, Mike?" I wanted to know how we were going to pull this off.

As always, Mike took charge. He said, "I'll take care of everything. Just like in the old days remember? I never let you down before, did I?"

I had to admit he was right. He always had my back where Johnny was concerned.

"Who's the third person?" I asked.

"The minister, or whoever is going to marry us," Mike laughed. "Okay," Mike went on, "I'll wait a couple weeks and tell him that you and I are seeing each other. Then we can figure out how long to wait before I tell him we're getting married."

It sounded like a showstopper. Better than any performance I could imagine. If we could pull it off, that is.

"Sleep on this Becky, you'll see that I'm right." He winked as he went out the door.

Emily and I just looked at each other. Could this possibly work? The bigger question was, "Did I want it to work? Did I even want Johnny if I could have him?"

It was working out on the other end. Mike had figured out the timeline and told Johnny, right on schedule, that we were seeing each other. He said Johnny swore at him big time. It would become much worse a couple weeks later when Mike announced that we were getting married. He said he thought Johnny was going to explode he was so upset.

33
Final Show: Savannah

We had found out a few weeks before we scheduled the mock wedding that the Silver Eagles and the Special Forces parachute team would be performing in nearby Savannah on a Saturday in July. For some reason Mike had insisted that the "wedding" be the same day as the show. I thought it was good planning, thinking we could watch some of the show from my condo. Savannah was only about sixty miles away. So we scheduled it for the third Saturday in July.

Mike would be bringing his son along to be "best man". They arrived early in the afternoon. The "wedding" was scheduled for 3 pm. Emily made sure that there were flowers everywhere. The beautiful scent of roses filled the air. It looked like a real wedding to me. It was a beautiful sun-filled day and the many colors of roses with the backdrop of the ocean made the deck look so pretty. We took lots of pictures.

Emily insisted I wear a knee length, off white, strapless dress. I felt like a real bride. My hair was elegant... long and straight, instead of up in my usual ponytail. Emily wore an exceptionally pretty green blouse and skirt, which looked fabulous with her auburn hair and green eyes. We both wore daisies in our hair. Mike looked very handsome in a light colored sport jacket and blue shirt. No tie. He was always so easy-going about everything. Even his "wedding".

At 2:45, the "minister" showed up. He was a friend of Mike's and while he thought we were all crazy, he was willing to play the game. He said hello to us while rolling his eyes and smirking. Mike's son, Brandon, was waiting up by the road. He was going to text us if Johnny showed up.

I was very nervous about all this. As the minutes ticked by, I was becoming more and more sure that this whole thing would be a bust. Johnny was nowhere in sight, but Mike wasn't giving up. "I just know he's going to do something. I know this guy. Watch and see."

At 3:05, I told Emily this was a joke. "Let's go have a drink at the club and forget this stupid stunt." Suddenly, we all heard aircraft high in the sky and looked up. Mike said, "What the hell!?" We couldn't see much, only a door that opened on the side of the hovering plane.

Mike started to yell, "I knew it, I knew

it!" as someone jumped. "Wait," he said, "Look! There are two people there. They're attached to each other! Somebody must be in training or something!" It was the parachute team's aircraft and the person that jumped was one of the team members.

I felt like we were on a movie set. "Emily, is this for real?" I asked. She nodded not making a sound, her eyes riveted on the jumper. Finally the yellow parachute opened. It drifted down towards us. Emily and I were speechless and I still didn't understand what was going on. We watched as the men landed safely on the beach in front of the condo, took off their garb and untangled the parachute. One of them walked directly towards us. My heart skipped a beat as I realized it was Johnny. Johnny Munroe. The man who claimed he would never consider thinking about jumping, let alone actually doing it. I remembered his words.

He glanced my way as he walked over to Mike and screamed in his face. "You can't marry her, you son of a bitch. You knew I would never let you do this." I thought he was going to punch him out. Mike was having trouble speaking. I could tell he never expected anything like this. He managed to say, "You outdid yourself this time, Johnny. I

———

232

knew you'd never let her go again."

Johnny then walked over to me and took both of my hands in his. He smiled and told me I looked beautiful. I was speechless. I just stared at him in disbelief.

"Listen to me, Becky, please," he pleaded. "I love you. This is for real you know. I couldn't let you marry Mike. I couldn't. Not when I know you still love me after all these years. You do still love me, don't you?"

My heart melted, but I couldn't find my voice. I looked at Johnny's face and realized he had been telling the truth all along. The truth was that he still had feelings for me. He insisted that he had tried to call me years ago but was told I had married someone else.

I finally whispered weakly, "You're right, of course, I've always loved you Johnny." The whispers inside of me came alive.

There was some applause from nearby people who were watching. We had gained an audience. I didn't hear much of what was going on around us. My attention was on Johnny. It was like time was standing still and we were two kids again, crazy in love. He took my hand and we walked down the beach together past the beach club. More people waved and clapped. They must have been wondering what on earth was going on.

Johnny started talking about all the things we were going to do together and what a great life we were going to have. "We'll make up for all those lost years, I promise," he said. "I'm so happy that you believe in me again." He was so proud of himself because he thought he had magically erased all the pain and disappointment from the past.

I was beginning to realize I was not the same Becky who was in love with him before. Something made me turn around and look back at Mike and Emily who were still standing back on the deck watching us. I could feel Mike's eyes burning a hole straight through me. The whispers inside me could not be ignored. I looked over at Johnny. Something wasn't right. Something just wasn't right! I shook my head and cried out with emotion that even surprised me.

"No, no. Wait! I've made a terrible mistake! It's not that simple. I'm not that person anymore!" I let go of his hand, took off my shoes and started running as fast as I could toward Mike and Emily. It was a miracle I didn't fall flat on my face.

Stunned, Johnny yelled, "Becky don't go, what are you doing? Where are you going?"

Mike saw me running back up the beach and he raced down the shoreline to meet me there. He picked me up, swung me around and said, "Becky, Becky, I fell for you at that first air show. But you and Johnny were always together. There was nothing I could do."

"What are you saying Mike?" I didn't understand.

He was so emotional as he explained how he had fallen for me the first time he laid eyes on me. I vaguely remembered how he kept staring at me as he walked back and forth in front of me at that first show. He knew there was no chance for us because he had a wife and kids at home. He realized as time went on it wouldn't have mattered anyway because I was so madly in love with Johnny. He planned the wedding stunt to be sure that after all these years I didn't still love him. He had to know for sure before he was honest about his feelings for me.

In that moment a lot of things started to make sense. Mike had a big heart. That's why he was always looking out for me. He wanted me to be happy even if it was with Johnny and not him. I glanced back toward the place where Johnny had been standing. He was nowhere in sight.

Mike and I walked hand in hand toward Emily who was staring at us trying to smile.

Tears were streaming down her face. For a moment we stopped and looked into each other's eyes. Mike held my face in his hands and kissed me. Our first kiss. We were lost in each other, completely oblivious to everything around us.

Suddenly the scream of jet engines jerked our faces upward. Out of seeming nowhere, the Silver Eagles flew in formation over us and headed out to sea. Everyone held their breath. It was dramatic and powerful. No one dared move. The silver and blue aircraft then circled back and made another pass over the beach, tipping their wings in a final salute. It was a final salute just for us.

With peace in our hearts, Mike and I watched transfixed until the planes were completely out of sight. The whispers were silent. All was well.

Sooner or later, love always finds a way.

About the Author

Retired after a long career with the airlines, author Joanne Patterson now enjoys life with her three shelties and spending time with good friends and family. A passion for animals and holistic medicine led her to become an Animal Reiki practitioner and for the past two decades she has treated and helped animals in need. For the past several years Joanne has been an active blogger on Facebook as well as facilitating a live daily commentary on a popular television soap opera. She has many devoted followers who enjoy her descriptive dialogue and join in with comments of their own.

Throughout her life she has traveled far and wide. She currently resides in Upstate New York where she loves the change of seasons and the beautiful countryside.

Thank you for reading! Please consider leaving us a review on Amazon if you have enjoyed our book!
You can continue to follow Becky on her Facebook page at
www.facebook.com/rebeccasteelechasingadream